WHAT IF History of Australia

COLONIAL SETTLEMENT

France vs Britain

www.bigskypublishing.com.au

By Craig Cormick Illustrated by Cheri Hughes

First published 2022

Big Sky Publishing Pty Ltd

PO Box 303, Newport, NSW 2106, Australia

Phone: 1300 364 611
Fax: (61 2) 8330 9211

Email: info@bigskypublishing.com.au

Web: www.bigskypublishing.com.au

Cover Design and Typesetting: Cheri Hughes

Printed in China.

Author: Craig Cormick

Title: What If History of Australia Colonial Settlement

ISBN: 9781922615763 (paperback)

Subjects: Middle Grade Fiction.

WHAT IF History of Australia

COLONIAL SETTLEMENT

France vs Britain

CONTENTS

CHAPTER 1

What If

What If Napoleon Bonaparte had been Emperor of Australia? Or What If Captain Cook had never gotten back to England to report on what he had found? Or What If the Spanish had settled Australia instead of the British?

What type of school might you now be going to and what language might you now be speaking?

These are all examples of What If histories. Imagining What If something else had happened in history and things had turned out very differently.

Pick any point in history and you can imagine another way that history might have gone. There are endless What If possibilities. Like What If the Roman Empire had never been defeated and took over the world, and we now all spoke Latin?

Or What If the Japanese and Chinese had combined forces during World War Two and invaded the USA and all our appliances and things were now made in China or Japan. Oh – hang on, all my appliances are made in China or Japan. Maybe that's not such a great example.

What about What If we ran out of petrol and all our energy had to be obtained from farts? We'd be fine at my place, but I don't know about yours.

Anyway, I'm sure you get the idea.

But the What If history we are going to talk about is What If Australia had been settled by the French instead of the British.

I'm sure you all know the standard story, that Captain Cook charted the east coast of Australia in 1770 and despite nearly sinking when he hit the Great Barrier Reef, he got back to England to tell everyone what he had found. He said the land was pretty good and that Botany Bay was an excellent place to build a city that could grow to become so overcrowded it would take hours to get to school in the traffic – but the beaches would be awesome.

Well, to be honest, what he actually said was that the land was hilly with mostly sandy soil, and the people he saw were "far more happier than we Europeans," living in tranquility with the environment.

And then the English politicians decided to do something either incredibly dumb or incredibly clever, and they chose to set up a penal settlement there. The First Fleet, with 11 ships, arrived in 1788 at Botany Bay, and established a settlement at Sydney Cove. Not at Botany Bay, which it turned out was not quite as excellent a place for starting a city as Cook had described it. He might have known a lot about oceans and making maps, but clearly he didn't know so much about the types of land best-suited for a settlement.

But you don't need to be reminded of that, do you, because you're undoubtedly the type of cool kid who knows a bit about history. And you also probably don't need to be reminded that the settlers never asked for permission to settle on the lands of the Gadigal people there – they just took the land and pushed the local people out.

You probably also know that the first few years of settlement were really hard with the colony nearly starving as they couldn't figure out how to grow food very well. And they didn't understand the First Nations people – despite kidnapping some and trying to teach them English and so on, without really learning much of their languages and culture. So it was a bit of a miracle that they finally got their act together and started prospering. First through agriculture and free settlement, using convict labour, and then through the gold rushes of the 1850s and 1860s.

The population kept growing and growing and everyone was doing better and better, and living a lifestyle that was far more happier than most Europeans, and most Australians were generally living in tranquility with the environment.

But of course the cities just kept on growing bigger and bigger until eventually people were living a lifestyle far more stressful than many Europeans, and damaging the environment.

And we are all now standing around wondering how did that happen? And What If we had done a few things differently?

CHAPTER 2

Enter Captain Cook

So let's play What If.

What If when Captain Cook's ship the *Endeavour* hit the Great Barrier Reef off the coast of north Queensland in 1770, his ship sunk instead of being repaired at the town now called Cooktown? What If he never got back to England to tell people that Botany Bay would be an excellent place to build a settlement?

Well that's where our first story starts, on 11 June 1770, up on the Great Barrier Reef.

So Cookie and his crew of Cookie Cutters have been cutting through the waters of the reef, wondering what they've gotten themselves into. I mean the first half of their trip up the coast of New South Wales seemed easy enough. They had cruised along making observations of the land, and "saw the smoke of fire in several places", which told them that people lived there.

And when they got to Botany Bay they put in and went ashore, waving cheap dollar shop trinkets for the locals as a way of welcome.

But the locals didn't want them, and waved spears back at them.

That led to one of the first games of beach volleyball in Australia, but instead of throwing a volleyball at each other, the locals threw a volley of spears and the British fired a volley of their muskets in return. One musket shot even wounded one of the locals in the leg and he had to hop off into the bush.

Peron

Almost the first game of hop, step and jump in Australia, but that record really goes to a crazy Frenchman named Francois Peron, who had landed in Tasmania in 1802, over 30 years later. To prove the French were superior to the locals they met he had planned to undertake all sorts of physical tests with them. Jumping, running and so on, as well as measuring their strength with a crazy device he had brought along called a 'dynanometre'. It was metal with strong springs and a dial and you had to pull and twist and squeeze it, and it took readings of how well you could pull and twist and squeeze things.

Peron used it to deduce that the Europeans were stronger than the locals. Of note, though, they chose not to compare spear throwing abilities!

Peron and his fellow French explorers then travelled north to Port Jackson, or Sydney Cove, and he wrote a rather strange account of how the French could invade and take over the colony with the help of rebellious Irish convicts.

That would be a great What If story in itself. But we are getting off the track of the main story.

The *Endeavour*: the truer facts

The *Endeavour* should more accurately be referred to as His Majesty's (HM) Bark *Endeavour*. This is because there was actually already a ship named His Majesty's Ship (HMS) Endeavor in commission in the Royal Navy at the time. Also Captain Cook had not yet achieved the rank

of Captain, and was only a First Lieutenant. And any ship captained by a First Lieutenant was referred to as a bark.

The ship was actually a converted coal ship, purchased by the navy, and was considered rather squat and ugly. But it did have a low keel – or bottom of the ship – so it was well-suited for navigating in shallow waters. Except when there was a low-lying reef there, of course!

~~Captain James Cook~~

Lieutenant James Cook

CHAPTER 3

The problem with coral reefs

So where were we? Oh yes, with Captain Cook (yeah yeah yeah, I know he was really only a First Lieutenant, but even though he was not a Captain [noun] in rank, he did captain [verb] the ship, and the crew all called him their captain [adjective, nouny thing]).

Thinking little of the complicated grammar involved, Cook captains the ship northwards and is soon enjoying the tropical warmth of Queensland, playing deck games with the crew and soaking up some warm rays of the sun. But he does not know that he is about to be trapped by the largest coral reef system in the world.

And when he finally does realise the danger all he can do is keep sailing along, with the coast on the left (port side) and the barrier reef on the right (starboard side), constantly seeking out a gap in the reef where the ship can escape back to the safety of the open seas.

The problem with coral reefs for a sailing ship in that time was that you could never really tell where the reefs were. Some you could see, and some might be hidden under the water, and especially at night you might not know they were there until you hit them.

And that is exactly what happened. On the night of 11 June, the *Endeavour* hit the reef and a great hole was knocked into the ship. They were very lucky though for a large chunk of coral got stuck in the hole, effectively plugging it, and one of the ship's crew, described a process he had seen on another ship where a spare sail was covered in animal poo and bits of untwisted rope and so on, and lowered over the side of the ship to make

a bandage to seal the leak. That sailor was midshipman Jonathon Monkhouse, whose brother was the ship's surgeon, William Monkhouse, whose job it was to put bandages on the crew when needed.

Anyway, that enabled them to sail the ship ashore where they beached it on the banks of the *Endeavour* River and were able to repair it and continue on their voyage.

James Cook: the truer facts

Born in Yorkshire, 1728

Died in Hawaii, 1779 (aged 50).

James Cook joined the Merchant Navy as a teenager, leaving school at 16, swapping over to the Royal Navy at the relatively late age of 26. Then he served around Canada, fighting the French. He did some pretty impressive surveying work of the Saint Lawrence River. Based on this he was given command of the *Endeavour* in 1766. His first of three major voyages was to take some scientists to Tahiti to observe the transit of Venus crossing the sun, and then in his spare time to find and map any big chunks of land he might find on the way home. He mapped New Zealand and the east coast of Australia.

His second voyage of the Pacific onboard the *Resolution* was to find a giant land mass further south of Australia. He proved no such land mass existed.

His third voyage was to find a northwest passage to Europe across the top of America. But he found the way as impassable as other navigators did, but mapped the coast of Alaska and the Bering Strait. He spent much time at Hawaii, where after initial good relations he may have overstayed his welcome and things turned nasty. Cook was killed, and parts of him sacrificially – well – cooked! Some remains were returned to his crew though, and the Hawaiian people seemed to regret what had happened.

He charted more of the earth than anyone ever, and memorials and monuments to him can be found right across the Pacific.

CHAPTER 4

Making a hit on the reef

So let's ask What If that big chunk of coral had not plugged the leak and What If nobody had ever seen that method of sealing a leak with a sail covered in poo and old rope, and What If the waves knocked the *Endeavour* onto the reef again and again, smashing it to bits?

There have been plenty of other ships that happened to on the Great Barrier Reef. Some sunk within hours and the crew had to abandon ship and try to make it to a nearby island or ashore. For the crew of the *Endeavour* they hit the reef in the middle of the night and it would have been chaos. People running around shouting and not knowing what to do and the ship tilting as it was bashed to bits and maybe the masts falling down and tangling everything in ropes.

But before we go too far with that story, I want to ask you if you might think sailing the Pacific Ocean onboard a sailing ship like the *Endeavour* would be a lot of fun?

CHAPTER 4

Well I can tell you that it isn't quite as much fun as you might think. It is a lot of hard work, with hot days and cold nights and broken sleep and seasickness and wanting to just get home again.

And I know that because in researching this book I actually signed up as a crew member on board the *Endeavour* replica, and did sail around a little bit of the Pacific Ocean on board it. And this is what it's like – you hop on board while the ship is at anchor and you feel the soft rocking of the ship and the smell of the wood and the rope and the tar that seals the planks and you think this is awesome!

CHAPTER 4

Until the ship sets sail and you get outside the harbour mouth and start pitching around on the open seas. Then the deck tilts and rocks and you feel your stomach tilting and rocking with it. And if you're lucky you'll be down on the ship pulling ropes and blistering your hands, but if you're not so lucky you might be up in the rigging, having climbed up the rope ladders and dragged yourself over the platforms on the masts and up higher, and up more ropes and over another platform, and then you edge out along the spar that holds the sail, with your feet on a wobbly rope below you and hanging on for dear life.

And you might be trying to let the sail down, untying some tough and salty knots as the ship pitches. And if you can't get the knots undone someone will be shouting at you and calling you a landlubber or something worse. Particularly if you spew up on them and it hits them on the deck, which is so far down below that it looks like you might be a thousand feet up in the air.

And eventually you might get to climb down to the deck again, but there will be another job for you to do. And it will probably involve going down under the deck and bumping your head on one of the low beams there, or slipping in someone else's spew.

And there is another and another difficult job to do until it is finally bedtime. And there isn't even a bed. It's a hammock slung from the ceiling under the deck. You are all packed in there like sardines – though if you wake up in the night and look around you'll see all the hammocks swinging together in perfect unison, like they are rocking and rolling as one. But in fact they aren't really moving – the ship is rocking and the hammocks are still.

And yes, you can still throw up when you are in a hammock, like you can throw up when you are on the ship's toilet or climbing a rope or anywhere at all. I suppose if you're at sea for several months you'd get used to it, but if not, for most of the trip you'll be thinking you can't wait to get onto dry land again. Unless of course you hit a reef and your ship sinks, then you'll be thinking that you wish you were on the ship still.

And that's just what Cook's men all thought when they hit the reef.

CHAPTER 5

That sinking feeling

So Captain Cook[1] is trying hard to restore order as the ship's deck tilts under his feet and his voice is drowned out by the roar of the surf against his ship and the reef, and by the awful groaning of his ship's timbers as they splinter. Then there are the desperate cries of the crew, who know they are going to sink.

If he can maintain order, he thinks, they will have a chance of surviving this. If they can lighten the ship. If they can keep the pumps working. If they can stem the flow of water. If the damage isn't too bad. If the wind drops and the sea calms.

He puts on his stern eyebrow face and starts issuing orders.

But it is too many ifs and it needs more luck than he has with him tonight. The ship's deck tilts even further beneath his feet and he shouts out, 'Lighten the ship!'

1 Yeah, yeah, yeah. I know. First Lieutenant Cook really. But let's just go with Captain Cook.

Those crew who are panicking light lanterns to "lighten" the ship. Those who are not panicking throw everything they can overboard. Barrels and stores and the ballast stones in the ship's hold and the ship's cannon and all the cases and boxes they can find.

CHAPTER 5

Joseph Banks, the ship's wealthy young botanist, is trying to stop the men throwing any of his things overboard. Even though all his things probably weigh as much as all the things of the rest of the ship combined. He has musical instruments and enough books to start a library and a zillion botanical samples and more clothes than you could wear in two years. And let's say he also had a collection of Greek statues of himself, and a full-length mirror and a life-sized painting of himself and 426 pairs of shoes and 120 barrels of fine wine and a four-poster bed and the stage props of just about every Shakespeare play ever written and – well you get the idea before this version of the story gets too silly.

He had just about everything you could squeeze onto a ship except for a grand piano. And he had tried to bring one, but no one could figure out how to fit it on board.

'Save my specimens,' he is shouting, walking along the deck holding a stuffed emu.

But no one is listening to him. Some men have gone below and smashed open the rum barrels, passing the drink around to their mates, thinking there is nothing better to do in such a predicament than get drunk. Which isn't really good advice, as history shows that while it might feel there are some situations that are so bad it surely wouldn't do any worse harm to go and get drunk – the opposite actually usually proves to be true.

CHAPTER 5

You know that primary school song, “What will we do with the drunken sailor?” Well there’s a verse you might not know, that goes:

‘If the ship’s sinking, he’ll drown firsto!’

There’s a good life lesson there!

Anyway, other members of the crew are trying to get the boats away, knowing they need to get them clear of the wreckage that is forming on the deck. The masts have already snapped and are all a tangle of ropes and spars and things, and if they fall any lower across the deck they will trap the boats there and no one will be able to get them free.

‘Hurry!’ the men all scream at each other, before realising that they are all doing the screaming and none of them are doing the pushing of the boats. So they change over quickly.

However there are actually not enough boats for the 90 or so men onboard. So while some work to get them free others just hurl hatch covers into the water as makeshift rafts and jump in after them. The sailors know well which things will float and which will not, as the disaster of a ship sinking is something they all carry in their dreams. No one clings to the cannon or to Joseph Banks’ many marble statues. But his stuffed animals look like they might float though and a few men go over the side riding on a kiwi, a wombat or his emu.

Interestingly, these stuffed animals float better than you might think.

Many sailors can't swim – which you'd think would be right up the top on their job selection criteria, along with pulling ropes without spewing, and looking for pirates. They are very reluctant to jump overboard and so they either run about the ship in panic or they climb up what remains of the rigging, hoping somehow it will keep them safe above the dark and perilous waters as the ship sinks.

CHAPTER 5

Yet history shows this is rarely a very sound strategy in a shipwreck.

Cook has grabbed hold of the ship's doctor, William Monkhouse, and tells him, 'Fetch your medical kit and supplies. We will need to get aboard one of the boats before the crew launch them.' The doctor is trying to tell the Captain something his brother has suggested, about using a sail as a bandage to plug the leak, but Cook thinks they have passed the time where any such schemes could be helpful. He tells the doctor again, 'Quickly. Fetch your things. And tell the other officers and naturalists to be prepared to leave the ship.'

Joseph Banks is then by his side, requesting that the Captain provide him with men to carry all his scientific samples up on deck. Cook knows that most of them have already been carried up – and thrown overboard. So he tells Banks he will see what he can do.

Then Cook says, 'But we must give priority to food and water.'

Banks says, 'But surely you can find food and water ashore. We must bring my botanical samples. They are priceless.'

'If we can eat them you can bring them,' Cook says.

Then Cook sees the men struggling with the larger of the ship's three boats have gotten it free and are lowering it to the water. 'Hop aboard,' he tells Banks. 'Or stay here with your botanical collections. You choose.'

Banks makes the quick and sensible type of decision you tend to make when you haven't breached the ship's rum barrel. He hops aboard the boat.

The evacuation of the ship is chaotic. Eventually, as the sun has begun lightening the sky to the east the ship's three boats are in the water. The men still on board the ship look around desperately for a nearby island that they might swim to. But there is nothing but the distant dark outline of the mainland – some 12 kilometres or so away.

And of course they can also see the boats, the rafts and men riding on stuffed animals making their long slow trip to the mainland. You can imagine the looks on their faces as they realise they can't even float ashore on the empty rum barrels because they smashed them open.

They know their story is not going to end well.

Eventually Cook and his sorry-looking surviving crew drag themselves ashore near the mouth of a nearby river. Some men step onto the solid ground and kiss it, having thought they'd never reach it alive. Others lay on the grass and weep, convinced they will die in this unknown place.

Cook stares around him cautiously, assessing the land and its potential to support them.

'What should we do?' one of the men asks him.

'Assemble the provisions and start making shelters,' Cook says. It is late in the day and they will need to row back out to the wreck tomorrow to rescue whatever men and supplies are still there. But they will need shelter here first.

CHAPTER 5

They don't know this land and don't know the people who might live here, so they turn to things they do know – tents and a cup of tea! They search around their supplies and find that they have neither. The small sails of the boats can be made into a tent of sort. But no tea! That is a disaster for any 18th century gentleman.

'Should we make a stockade?' the man asks. 'In case of hostile natives?'

Cook considers that and remembers the confrontation at Botany Bay. 'Yes,' he says. 'A sound suggestion.'

'Can we make a gazebo for my plants?' asks Banks. He has managed to carry a few specimens ashore. 'They will grow much better under a gazebo?'

'I think the stockade first,' says Cook, putting on his stern eyebrow face.

CHAPTER 6

Exit Captain Cook

Now here's a thing – if you set your mind to believe something, it is quite likely going to feel true. So if in our story Captain Cook[2] and his crew think that the local people might be hostile to them, and if they build a fort and constantly carry what weapons they have to defend themselves, you can be assured that when they see any locals they will expect violence from them.

You may have heard the saying that if you have a hammer, then everything looks like a nail. Well likewise, when you have guns everything looks a bit like a target.

If, on the other hand, you expect the best of the locals and start behaving as if they will be peaceful, when you encounter them it is more likely to be a peaceful encounter.

So let's look at those two What Ifs.

2 Yes, yes, I know. He was not captaining a ship now so he should be just First Lieutenant here.

CHAPTER 6

If Cook has his men build a stockade – which is like a dollar shop version of a fort – and they all hide inside it and keep their few surviving muskets loaded and otherwise carry spears and clubs with them everywhere, the locals will see them and presume they are hostile and will keep their distance.

The Europeans will hunt and gather food and will shoot at animals and maybe even fire into the air when they see the locals, to scare them off, and the locals will consider them dangerous. They are not like the men they have seen who come from the islands to the north to trade with them.

They will eventually meet up, of course, and the meeting is not likely to go well. The Europeans are already a little scared of the dark men they see slipping through the trees at a distance, and they find spears and things in their abandoned camps, and know they have weapons.

Meanwhile the English discover many new plants and animals, much to Joseph Banks' delight, and just about every animal they see they shoot and eat. Kangaroos and birds and possums and dingoes. Banks wants to give a name to everything the hunting parties bring back to camp, but the men just want to call it dinner.

CHAPTER 6

Even if the Captain has entreated his men to treat any of the locals they see peaceably, if you're in the bush, a little scared, and you see a dark-skinned man with a spear, your first reaction might be to think of defending yourself, not seeking peace. And unfortunately this happens quite a lot in history.

The unknown generally feels scary.

It doesn't really matter how they meet, whether the locals want to confront the Europeans about the large amount of food they are killing and taking, or the way they are treating the land, or whether some of the Europeans come across a group of locals unexpectedly. There is confrontation and that leads to violence.

The Europeans of course believe they have the superior arms and tactics, but their gunpowder is very limited. They have skills in fighting a European war, but much less in fighting hit and run war. The locals, however, are very skilled in this, and can hunt silently and throw their spears with great force and accuracy.

And eventually it will come down to that. The gunpowder will run out and both sides will be throwing spears at each other. Wary of the other. Unable to communicate with the other through any other means than violence.

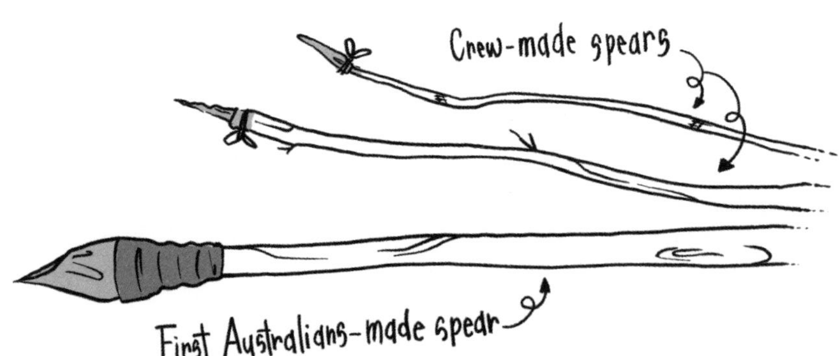

And of course it all ends badly. More so for the group with no real practice in building and throwing spears.

Cook and his crew have little chance of surviving if they cannot safely go into the forests for food. They have not saved enough supplies from the ship to last too long and when the rainy season comes they start getting sick with all kinds of diseases.

Along this path of our What If history, within three years of having come ashore there is not a single man left alive from the *Endeavour*.

CHAPTER 7

A better ending

But if we play the What If game another way, it might end up quite differently.

The Captain[3] and the crew struggle ashore and are exhausted. They are in an unknown land with unknown plants and animals all about them and have few supplies to live on. Many of the crew have either drowned on the wreck or while trying to come ashore, and the survivors cling together expecting their Captain will make sure they are all safe.

Cook has brought very little ashore apart from his navigation instruments and logbooks. He has not even brought a flag to plant somewhere. So his first order is to have shelters built for everyone. Then he has a supply store assembled and guards placed over it. He is not going to let the ill-discipline that occurred on the ship when it was sinking be repeated here and endanger them all.

3 I know, I know. And I'm sorry I even told you he was really a First Lieutenant!

Banks, meanwhile, draws up plans for a gazebo for his plants. He alone will be able to plant something here, even if it is not a flag. He lays out the few plants that he has saved and makes little paths between them lined by stones. He even imagines putting little garden gnomes around them. He is an 18th century English gentleman, let's remember.

The men spend their first few nights only half-sleeping, jumping at every sound they hear from the bush around them. Their first encounters with the natives at Botany Bay ended up in exchanging volleys of spears and musket fire, and Cook knows that they cannot retreat to the ship if they are attacked here.

'Keep an eye out, but do not provoke any violence,' he tells the guards.

But the men spend the night pointing their muskets at every noise they hear, ready to pull the trigger. One guard even shoots one of Banks' plants, mistaking it for somebody creeping up on him in the dark. The noise of the musket shot wakes everybody in a panic, of course and it takes some time to figure out it was a false alarm.

Cook knows they can't keep having nights like that and the next morning he determines to make contact with the locals and seek their help. With Joseph Banks and the Tahitian native who joined their ship in Tahiti, Tupaia, he goes into the bush to try and make contact.

CHAPTER 7

Tupaia had proved invaluable in communicating with the Maori of New Zealand, as he spoke a similar language. But the people who live here are certainly not Maoris and do not speak a language he might be able to understand.

Cook and co. spend all day stomping around in the bush, but the only native camp they find is deserted. So they head back to their own camp empty-handed.

Cook puts on his stern eyebrow face and helps Banks build his stone-edged paths. He'd paint them white if they had saved any paint from the wreck, he thinks.

Eventually Tupaia makes contact on his own. Although he does not understand any of the language of the locals, unlike in New Zealand, he does have a bit more of an idea about how to approach them than the Europeans do. He sits on the ground in a clearing, with gifts spread about him, and waits for the locals to come to him.

The first meeting is a success and he trades some trinkets for two fish.

The next day Cook comes with him. They sit on the ground for a long time, and Cook worries that no one is going to come, and they'll be sitting there all day looking like men stuck on the toilet. But eventually the locals come out of the bush, approaching them warily, and again the trade goes well.

Soon there is regular contact between Cook and his men and the local Guugu Yimidhirr people. Both groups realise they are going to have to come to some accord with the others and slowly, with a few steps forward and a few steps backwards, they discover how to live together.

It's not easy, of course, since they come from such different worlds with such different understandings of how the world works, and they value such different things. If the Europeans, for instance, go hunting, they consider the person who catches the animal the one who gets to choose the best pieces. The locals, however, have a much more communal view of food and how it should be shared.

Also the Europeans consider a home is somewhere you build a house and plant a garden, while the locals tend to roam all over their land with little consideration to any permanent structures or places. The Europeans try and understand the world through observation and scientific deduction and the locals have their own world views, formed through observing the world through a different lens. And of course the Europeans have no women and children, while the locals have both.

And that leads to a bit of awkwardness when Cook's sailors start getting just a little bit too friendly with the local women, as happened all over the world where a bunch of sailors who have been at sea for many months arrived, without ever having read a single book on feminism. Added to this is the fact that the women of Tahiti were so very friendly with the sailors, but that is not the locals' custom here.

And let's be honest, a European sailor in stinky sweat-soaked cotton or wool clothes that are starting to turn into rags in the rough bush, and who is not too used to baths, and probably has skin rashes and insect bites all over, and doesn't speak your language, probably wouldn't be any body's first choice for a date.

Anyway hostility is avoided through negotiation and some form of punishment is agreed upon for those who do wrong. The Europeans slowly learn what things are more acceptable and what are less acceptable to the locals, and how to survive in this land.

Under this What If scenario, when Europeans next arrive in the area, maybe 20 or so years later, they find some old men living with the locals who tell them they are European sailors. They show them the stone-lined gardens they have made and then explain the ways and beliefs of the locals, introducing each of the men and women by their names. Some even introduce their own children.

And some of the shipwreck survivors choose to stay, and some choose to leave, helping the newly arrived Europeans to better understand the First Nations people all over the continent.

It is a better ending for all along this alternative history path.

CHAPTER 8

A possum-o'-nine tails

Of course there are many, many different What If options you might imagine.

What if, for instance, Captain Cook[4] has trouble keeping control over his men, as many of them say that without a ship he has no authority over them. And without a well-armed troop of armed marines to keep order, the sailors stop paying attention to the orders Cook gives them.

And then they start forming their own little groups.

You can imagine one day Cook wakes up to find that 20 or so men are gone. He does his stern eyebrow thing and asks Joseph Banks if he knows where they are.

'Sorry,' says Banks. 'I didn't realise anyone was missing. I was counting my new botanical specimens. And they are all still here you'll be pleased to know.'

'No, I'm not particularly pleased to know that. I want to know where the missing men have gone.'

4 Enough already!

'I'm sure they'll turn up.'

'I think that's what you said in Tahiti when the men ran away, and we had to send soldiers into the interior to find them and bring them back.'

'Ah, yes, Tahiti,' says Banks. 'Now that was something worth running away for.'

'Are you saying that you would have run off and taken up with a Tahitian maiden like the sailors had?'

'Uh – no, not at all. I meant the botanical specimens there. I could have spent many, many months exploring them.'

'I see. And what do you think of the botanical specimens here?'

'Quite amazing. There are flowers and plants here that are completely unknown in Europe. If I could bring just a few dozen of these back to England I'd be the toast of the Royal Society.'

'If I could bring just a few dozen of our men back I'd be the toast of the Admiralty. But that's not going to happen if they keep running away.'

'Why don't you ask Doctor Monkhouse. He seems to have a fair grasp of what's going on.'

'I don't think any of us really have much of a grasp of what is going on here,' Cook sighs.

So Cook goes exploring and discovers that the missing men have set up a stockade of their own, up on the hill overlooking the small settlement they all call, mockingly, Cooktown. He goes up to order them to return – which is a lot easier said than done as it can get pretty humid in Cooktown, trust me on this. And if you go for a walk in the heat of the day and try and walk up a hill, you'll be sweating like a – well, like an Englishman trying to walk up a hill in the humid heat of the day. Especially if you're wearing your woollen Captain's coat as a mark of authority. The heat and humidity saps all the energy out of you and you just want to lie down somewhere cool and sleep.

I know this, because in researching this book I went all the way up to Cooktown and climbed up that hill so that I could tell you all exactly what it felt like.

Well, when I say I climbed up that hill, I mean I drove up most of it in a car, but I did hike up the last little bit to the top, you know, to get the feeling of it.

And when I say I hiked the last little bit to the top, what I really meant was that I walked from the car park along the path to the picnic area at the top. But I was thinking this is how Cook would have done it (if he had a car and a road and a footpath, you know).

Well Cook gets to the top of the hill and the men there tell him that he isn't their Captain anymore and can't order them about.

'That's mutinous talk,' he says. 'I'll have you all flogged.'

CHAPTER 8

'No you won't,' their leader says. 'You ain't even got a cat-o'-nine tails to whip us with.'

'I'll make one,' Cook says, wondering what a possum-o'-nine tails might be like.

'You'd be better off if you could make us a boat so that we could all escape from here,' they tell him. 'That camp of yours down by the river is useless. You are too close to the natives. They'll creep up and slit your throats one night. We are staying put here. And if a ship happens to pass by we'll spy it and be able to light a fire to signal it. We will be the ones that save us.'

But Cook shakes his head and gives the men his sternest eyebrow look. 'No ship has ever sailed this way before we did, so what makes you think one will come past now?'

Cook asks. 'And even if a ship did come past, it would too far out at sea to spy a fire. The reefs are too thick and too dangerous for a ship to come in closer.'

The men all look out to sea. They can see the pale blue of shallows and the white breakers where the surf is breaking across reefs and that seems to stretch forever. There may be something in what Cook says, but they reply, 'You're just saying that to trick us to come back. We have had enough of the Royal Navy. We are now our own men.'

'Then you will likely die your own men!' Cook says.

'You will die before us. Mark my words,' they tell him.

But Cook is right in this. There are enough empty ruins of forts and stockades around the world to show that trying to live apart from the local people without being resupplied from Europe is not a sound way of staying alive.

CHAPTER 9
Exit Captain Cook again

Cook storms back to the camp and finds that others are now mumbling about leaving, like it's the end of the tourist season or something. The men are growing concerned that there is not enough food in the area to continue to feed them all. Already the fish in the river have become scarce. There is concern that the locals might turn on them at some time too. There is concern that someone might steal the remaining boat. Already they have lost one when some men went fishing and struck another reef, caving in the bottom of the boat and five men drowning.

Cook is not ready to risk the remaining boat just yet though. It is all he has as a symbol of his authority over the men. And it will need to be made more seaworthy, but they lack the tools to make new planks. He had at one time thought to salvage wood from the wreck of the *Endeavour* – but it has been pounded into pieces on the reef. There is no visible sign that they have even been there.

Those calm placid waters out there can be savage in a storm and they have erased all signs of the *Endeavour*. The heat and the mosquitoes and the need to adapt to so many new things beyond his training is wearing him out and he sleeps fitfully that night, dreaming that terrible dream – that he has gone to school without any pants on!

The next morning Cook wakes to find five more men are gone. They have stolen supplies and snuck off in the night. You can picture the disappointed look on his face as tries vainly to do his eyebrow thing and asks, 'Have they gone to join the others on the hill?'

'No. They are determined to walk to freedom. They are convinced that if they walk along the coast they will sight a ship somewhere and be saved.'

But the locals have already told Tupaia that if they travel too far north they will encounter bad people who are likely to attack them. Cook has no belief that he will even see these missing men again, nor will anyone else.

Nor does he really understand that the people who live around him are not the same as the people at Botany Bay.

Slowly, though, he learns new words and new concepts and begins to understand that the Guugu-Yimidhirr people live on the land north of the river and those to the south are the Kuku-Yalanji. And he learns that the shipwreck survivors have somehow, fortunately, landed at a piece of land that is like a neutral territory between the two peoples.

And he learns that further to the west are the Kokowarra people, and he learns that there are another ten or so language groups of people to the north until the land finally becomes the empty ocean.

As the men with him slowly reduce in numbers through accidents or running away, the few remaining crew members are taken in by different clan groups. They teach them to live with the land and how to find foods in different seasons. And as the bush slowly grows over their stockades, the Europeans settle into the families and tribes they are living with, slowly becoming more a local than a European.

Then, when a ship finally lands here again, 30 or 40 years later, they are surprised to find some people with red or blond hair and green and blue eyes. But of Captain Cook and his crew, there are only stories remaining.

CHAPTER 10

Exit Captain Cook a final time

Now here's something to consider. We could extend our What If story so that after coming ashore from the wreck some of the crew take the best boat and sail it all the way to Batavia (now Indonesia) to get help. It's a long trip in an open boat, but not impossible. Captain Bligh sailed further when he was put off the *Bounty* into a small boat by mutineers in 1789. And the survivors of the *Pandora* that sank on the reef further north of Cooktown in 1791 (searching for the *Bounty* mutineers in fact), also made it to Batavia in a small open boat.

But that isn't going to suit our next What If story, if someone brings back help. We want to explore a path in which Cook and his men disappear from history.

So sorry First Lieutenant James Cook, if someone does take a boat and try and make their way north they are wrecked in a storm, or their boat sinks some other way, or they are abducted by aliens (okay, not that last one), and the shipwreck survivors left behind slowly die out or integrate with the local people until they are effectively out of our telling of the rest of the story. Captain Cook

Bligh's 6,700 kilometre open boat journey to Batavia

becomes another explorer missing in action and never heard from again.

And then we can turn to what might happen next.

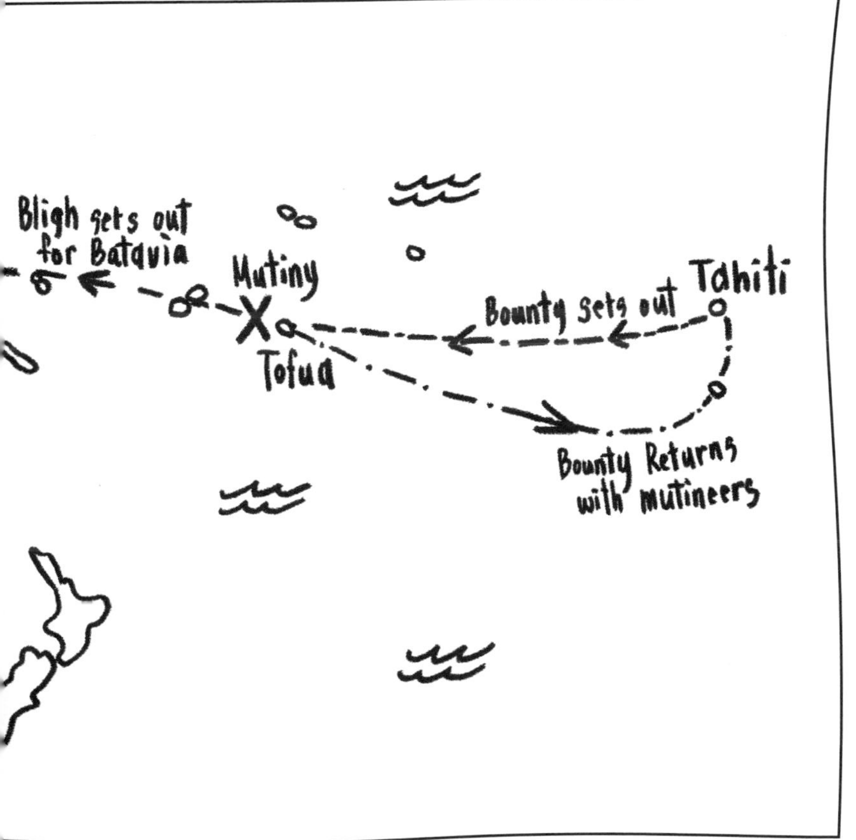

CHAPTER 11

Enter the French

Now back to the French. You might not know this, but when the real First Fleet actually arrived in Botany Bay in 1788, two French Ships, under the command of Jean François de Galaup, the Count of La Perouse, arrived there a few days later.

The British and French exchanged pleasant greetings and after a few weeks the French sailed away – and disappeared. And they were never seen again.

That has often been used as the basis of saying, 'Wow, if the First Fleet had arrived a few days later the French would have beaten us and we'd all be French. Mon Dieu!' (Which is how they say OMG in French).

Well that's probably over-stating things, as La Perouse was there exploring, not looking to set up a settlement.

La Perouse was an interesting man, despite looking like he had just done a fart which had taken him by surprise and startled him.[5]

5 A 'fartle'.

CHAPTER 11

Jean François de Galaup, or La Perouse

He had fought against the British in Canada (like Cook, but on the other side) and distinguished himself so well he was promoted and promoted again (like Cook), eventually becoming a Commodore. He also broke convention by marrying a young Creole, or mixed race woman, from Mauritius, named Louise-Eléonore Broudou, (not like Cook).

Her portraits show her with a small mouth, small chin, small nose and huuuuuge hair.

Louise-Eléonore Broudou

Anyway, La Perouse was 43 years old when he was given the task of undertaking an exploration voyage around the world, in 1785 (to prove the French could do exploration things just as well as the British). The first thing he did was to recruit competent people. One of the applicants was a very ambitious 16-year-old Corsican Second Lieutenant from Paris's military academy, named Napoleon Bonaparte. He made the short list, but was ultimately not selected, and that leads to a whole other What If question. What If Napoleon had gone with La Perouse and disappeared down the plug hole of history and Europe never had a Napoleon to influence events?

As I said, La Perouse wasn't really interested in claiming the land of New South Wales, for his mission was to complete the work of Captain Cook (but in a French way) and discover new scientific things for France to gloat about. So the French went ashore at Botany Bay and built a small stockade (a dollar shop version of a fort, remember), to protect themselves from the locals.

Then they built an observatory, made scientific observations, and planted gardens on shore. And, like Captain Cook, 18 years earlier, they buried one of their dead crewmen there.

Of interest, La Perouse and Governor Arthur Phillip never met in person, but there were plenty of other visits between the French and English officers and sailors.

We don't know too much about the French encounters with the local people, because we don't have the records they might have kept. But the French stayed at Botany Bay for six weeks, which might have been enough to gain the trust of the local people and communicate with them – however we'll never know. In one of the letters La Perouse had sent back to France with the British, he wrote: "They threw spears at us one minute after receiving our present and signs of friendship."

The French were also said to have turned back a few convicts that escaped from Sydney Cove and made their way over land to try and hitch a ride to freedom with them.

They finally waved au revoir to the British and sailed off to the north-east and promptly disappeared off the map, like a very small toy boat going down the bath plug hole.

In fact it is now known that his ships ran aground on the reefs of one of the Solomon Islands – much as our What If Cook did on the Great Barrier Reef. The story goes that the men were then attacked by the locals, but some built a small boat from their wreck to escape. And they sailed away a second time and again promptly disappeared off the map. Like an even smaller toy boat going down the bath plug hole.

But the bit about the French that is most relevant to our What If history is that the French had actually been to Australia before Captain Cook – and just after him as well. In fact many Europeans had sighted bits of Australia before Captain Cook. They included:

- the Dutch navigator Willem Janszoon in 1606 (northern Australia)
- followed later the same year by the Spaniard Luís Vaez de Torres, whom the Torres Strait was named after (Torres Strait Islands)
- the Dutchman Dirk Hartog in 1616 (Western Australia)
- another Dutchman Frederik de Houtman in 1619 (Western Australia)
- the Englishman John Brooke in 1622 (north Western Australia)

- another Dutchman Jan Carstensz in 1623 (northern Australia)
- and yet another Dutchman François Thijssen, in 1627 (southern Australia)
- followed by another, Francesco Pelsaert in 1629 (Western Australia)
- and another Abel Tasman both in 1642 and in 1644 (Tasmania)
- and yet another, Willim de Vlamingh in 1696 (Western Australia)
- my uncle Brian in 2010 – sorry, just testing if you're paying attention.
- then another Englishman, William Dampier in 1688 (north western Australia)
- and the Frenchman Louis de Bougainville in 1768 (Great Barrier Reef).

So before Captain Cook reached Australia the score was roughly Holland 9, England 2, Spain 1 and France 1. Though there is an even earlier claim by Portugal, in the 1520s, waiting for the referees to adjudicate on. And there are even some Chinese claims that are considered by Europeans to be in a different playing league altogether, and are not generally counted.

Louis-Antoine de Bougainville

CHAPTER 12

The First French in Australia

Anyway – the first French explorer to sight Australia was Louis-Antoine, the Count of Bougainville – two years before Captain Cook (though technically he saw the waves breaking on the Great Barrier Reef and turned away to the north east, probably without ever sighting the mainland). But Bougainville had even more in common with Captain Cook than La Perouse did – despite looking a bit like your most scary old uncle with a wig on.

He fought the British in northern America, defending Quebec and the Saint Lawrence River, and earlier, in 1755 he had actually been in London as a secretary to the French Embassy. He even became a member of the British Royal Society – the scientific body that sponsored Cook's first voyage around the world to observe the transit of Venus in Tahiti.

Well, in 1776, at the age of 47, Bougainville was tasked with being the first Frenchman to circumnavigate[6] the

6 Sail right around the world better than the Spanish or English could.

globe, which was becoming a bit of a boasting trick at diplomatic parties. And the French were clearly getting a bit miffed by the English boasting, as they had no one who had done it.

There were some very interesting people onboard his ship, including a young Jean-François de Galaup de la Pérouse, and a valet to the botanist Philibert Commerçon who turned out to be his girlfriend dressed as a man – Jeanne Bare. She became the first woman known to circumnavigate the world.

Pretty cool if you ask me.

Bougainville visited Tahiti and claimed it for France and took onboard a Tahitian named Ahutoru (just as Cook had done with Tupaia). He then almost reached Australia, but rather than make such a hit on the Great Barrier Reef as Cook did, he instead reached the Solomon Islands, naming the island of Bougainville after himself. Then he headed back to France to be wheeled out at diplomatic parties to tell everyone how he had sailed right around the globe (and how he had done it better than the English or Spanish had).

Well that's all very interesting to know, of course, but the Frenchman we really want to talk about was Marc-Joseph Marion du Fresne. He was aged 48 and looked a bit like a grinning long-haired hippy in a nice coat.

CHAPTER 12

Marc-Joseph Marion du Fresne

He came along four years later, and only two years after Cook – in 1772. He landed in Tasmania and there is a bit of an interesting story about how he got there.

In short, he was helping that Tahitian native, Ahutoru, that Bougainville had brought to France, to return to his home in Tahiti.

Although du Fresne's luck wasn't much better than La Perouse's (who disappeared, remember) because first

Ahutoru died on the voyage, then two of du Fresne's ships crashed together. Then he landed in Tasmania hoping to get wood to repair them, but the locals threw rocks and things at them until they left for New Zealand.

His luck wasn't any better there. After initially getting on well with the Maori people they met, things turned nasty. They may have overstayed their welcome, or the Maori might not have wanted their trade goods or weapons or just didn't like the way they played football. The result was that that Maori attacked him and his crew and killed 25 men. Including Marc-Joseph Marion du Fresne himself!

Are you starting to see how much luck plays a role in who becomes famous and who doesn't? Or who disappears from history and who doesn't? And who gets gold-plated underpants for Christmas and who doesn't? (Okay, not that last one).

So let's ask a What If question. What If du Fresne wasn't as unlucky as La Perouse? What If he'd landed on the shores of Tasmania – and despite it already being named Van Diemen's Land by the Dutch, he renamed it New France?

But then he remembers that there was already a New France in North America (where Cook and Bougainville and so on had been fighting, you recall). So he names it New New France.

And What If when he came ashore, rather than carrying junk from some Paris dollar shop, he brought things that the locals were actually interested in trading for. Like, um, something French that was really, really cool that wasn't a stale French loaf or a beret. I mean there must have been something!

Well anyway, so the French spent some time ashore there and du Fresne said to his crew, 'Hey, I think this place would make an excellent site for a French colony, oui?'

And his crew said, 'Certainement!'[7]

So he sailed back to France, without getting killed in New Zealand, and told everyone about New New France. He said it would be great for holidays and the climate was really good for growing apples, and for hiking, and all the other wonderful things about Tasmania that have just escaped my mind at the moment, and recommended the French build a settlement there.

And the French officials said, 'Certainement!'[8]

7 Translation: Can we go home now?
8 Translation: We will beat the English this time!

CHAPTER 13

New New France

So in our What If history when La Perouse comes to Australia in 1788, he's now scouting out places for a settlement (and let's be frank, any settlement of land that is already occupied is just a much nicer way of saying an invasion). And rather than go to Botany Bay, he goes to Van Diemen's Land – sorry, New New France. But he arrives in winter and let's be honest, it can be a bit cold and rainy there in winter, and he thinks maybe du Fresne wasn't so clever at picking good land for a settlement, and he sails further north.

He goes across the Bass Strait, which of course would be the La Perouse Strait now, and he establishes the city of Melbourne! Which he calls Louisville, after King Louis the 16th of France.

Now before we get too far into our What If story of how the French settled the area we now know as Melbourne, we should know a few things about how the English settlement of it actually went.

The area was first explored by a Scotsman named John Murray in 1802 – though he did have a lot of trouble sailing into the mouth of Port Phillip Bay, and when he finally did get in the local people told him in no uncertain terms where they thought he should go. Back where he came from!

But he stayed about a month surveying the Bay and wrote of it, like he was a real estate salesman: "The southern shore of this noble harbour is bold high land in general and not clothed as all the land at Western Point is with thick brush but with stout trees of various kinds and in some places falls nothing short, in beauty and appearance, of Greenwich Park."

Greenwich Park is a place in England that is – well – a park!

Then an Englishman – Charles Grimes – showed up the next year and did another survey, discovering the Yarra River. Which makes you wonder what was John Murray doing there for a whole month if he didn't find the Yarra?

Possibly he was just sitting around on the beaches and having real estate dreams?

Anyway, after Charles Grimes' glowing recommendations and the discovery of a source of fresh water, you just know it wasn't going to be too long before somebody decided it would make a good place for a settlement.

And that guy was Lieutenant David Collins. Sort of. He went to Port Phillip Bay with 450 people (soldiers and settlers and 300 convicts) to establish a settlement that would stop the French landing there. But he clearly would have been a lousy real estate agent because he chose the area of Sullivan Bay, which is miles and miles away from where Melbourne ended up. It is just inside Port Phillip Bay on the right-hand arm of land that made the entrance to the Bay.

He might have thought it was a good strategic position to be able to show the French they had got there first, but it was a lousy place for a settlement. There wasn't much fresh water, nor suitable trees, nor holiday parks nor dollar shops. And also the difficult entrance to the Bay made it very hard to get supplies in. Added to that many of the convicts ran away.

So after only three months the settlement was abandoned, and they all moved to Van Diemen's Land. Except for the convicts who had run away of course.

And that's a whole other What If story.

I'm Batman!

CHAPTER 14

Batman

Then came John Batman. And what a guy he was. If we What If him, he might have been on track to become the colony's first crime-fighting superhero like his namesake. In fact, when he was a young blacksmith's apprentice in Sydney he dobbed in his boss for burglary. Then when he moved to Van Diemen's land he single-handedly captured the feared bushranger Matthew Brady.

Looking pretty good so far, yes?

And he took a very active part in tracking down Aboriginal Tasmanians, who the settlers were in fear of, and he was considered a bit of a hero by the locals for his efforts. Again, he was praised for his work. Then he went over to Port Phillip Bay and became the first person to enact a Treaty with the local people, when he traded goods for land in 1835.

A treaty! That has to be good, right, while everyone else was just stealing the land.

But John Batman, it turns out, was actually more like a Two-face villain than a Batman type hero. In tracking down Aboriginal Tasmanians he was ruthless, which was described by the then Governor as, he had "much slaughter to account for".

And his famous Treaty with the Wurundjeru people of Port Phillip wasn't as good as it sounds. He traded tools, blankets and food for thousands of hectares of land stretching from Melbourne to Geelong. The deal was not only very exploitative, but was something the locals did not fully understand. It has been argued that the Wurundjeru people probably saw the signing as something like their own Tanderrum ceremony, by which gifts were exchanged for access to, and use of, land – but not ownership of it. The gifts that Batman received were some stone axes, boomerangs and two fur cloaks – or capes.

Batman. Cape. Get it? Don't worry. Bad bat joke.

If you look up a picture of John Batman you'll see he looks more like a cocky bushranger than an explorer. And these days John Batman would be thought more of as a real estate con man, or a shonky land developer, but back in the 1840s he was described by one of his neighbours as a "rogue, thief, cheat and liar, a murderer of blacks and the vilest man I have ever known".

He had an odd idea of ownership of things too. For instance, he had previously kidnapped some younger First Nations boys and kept them on his farm, arguing they were now his property.

What a guy!

And that Treaty – which he modestly called the Batman Treaty – was not recognised by the colonial government. They weren't too happy about a free citizen doing deals with the locals for land. Something that hasn't much changed over the years since for most of our history it was the only treaty that was ever negotiated with the traditional owners of the land in Australia.

The details of the agreement were that eight Elders of the Kulin nation were agreeing to Batman renting their land on an annual basis for 100 pairs of blankets, 100 knives, 100 axes, 50 suits of clothing, 50 mirrors, 50 pairs of scissors and five tons of flour.

And in exchange he got 500,000 acres of land. Though it is worth noting that if the annual rent had actually continued to be paid from the agreement in 1835, by 2020 the Kulin people would have accumulated over 9,250 pairs of scissors!

It does sound a bit like giving away steak knives to encourage a sale like you might see on TV, I know.

But wait – there's more! In addition he was required to make an initial payment of 200 handkerchiefs, 100 knives, 50 pair of scissors, 40 blankets, 30 axes, 30 mirrors, 100 pounds of flour and six shirts.

He then staked out the land where the centre of Melbourne now stands as the ideal place for a village, and said it should be called Batmania!

What a guy! Though I think I mentioned that already?

And in case you don't yet quite get the point of what a terrible person he was, he also died of a sexually transmitted disease at the age of only 38. He spent his final years living in disfigured agony, a bit like the villain Two-face, I know. And perhaps most ironic of all, before his death he was cared for by some of the local First Nations people.

So before we progress with the story we can use our own What If superpowers to change his story and re-imagine John Batman as being the type of guy he wanted others to think he was.

What If that Treaty he signed with the First Nations peoples of Port Phillip was a fair document that recognised their rights and access to the land, and enabled him to farm it, without owning it, in a form of mutual cohabitation.

And What If while the colonial government still weren't happy about it, it became the basis for other treaties signed all around the country. Imagine settlers recognising the rights of the First Nations people to have access to their land, and they in turn would allow settlers to farm the land, providing some of their produce to the First Nations peoples for rent.

How differently might our history have played out then? How might the different peoples have found common interests if they could have found a common way to view and share the land and its resources?

It's a big What If, I know, but only slightly less crazy than imagining it would ever be possible to trade tens of thousands of hectares of land for some blankets, axes, mirrors, scissors and handkerchiefs.

Oh yes, and the scissors – the 19th century equivalent of steak knives!

CHAPTER 15

Louisville or Louiston or Chez Louis or something

Anyway – the whole point of the Batman story was that the local people of Port Phillip Bay – of the Kulin nation – were open to negotiations, rather than just throwing spears at new arrivals. And the French tended to be pragmatic – sometimes – and What If they started off trying to settle the land peaceably by making treaties with the locals?

And here is something else that is interesting to know, at that time there was this idea about the 'Noble Savages', that had been started by the French philosopher Jean Jacques Rousseau. It was based on the idea that primitive peoples were free from any notions of sin and greed and wrongdoing, that Europeans had, and that Europeans could learn a lot from them.

CHAPTER 15

If Rousseau had spent more time amongst indigenous peoples of the world, and less in books, he might have discovered there was a fair amount of fighting and wars and things like sin and greed and wrongdoing amongst them as well. But his ideas were a better way to consider the local inhabitants of a new country than just considering them primitive savages, as many others of the era did.

So, back to our story, La Perouse lands a few settlers at Port Philip – sorry, Louisville – and they find a nice place where they can build houses and plant trees and bake French loaves and whatever.

The French settlers try hard to establish good relations with the local people, and even try to learn some things from them. But to be honest, the French aren't too much better at this than the English. Despite their best intentions too many of the locals catch European diseases or are chased off their land by aggressive settlers, and when they complain about it the French soldiers decide the best thing to do is to march out and shoot at them.

If that's sounding too much like what happened around Sydney Cove, let's What-If-ify it instead. What If one of the settlers was really dark-skinned, like he or she had come from the Caribbean or somewhere. And What If he or she hadn't read too much of Rousseau's idealised ideas of noble savages, but was more grounded in reality. And What If he or she was really interested in languages and before too long was acting as translator between the settlers and the First Nations people? What If they ended up living mostly peacefully alongside each other?

Wouldn't that be something?

What If, when there was a dispute, they talked about it to figure out an answer? And What If the settlers started using indigenous ways of tending the land, rather than trying to force European ways onto it?

What kind of a society might that have been?

But of course there are also less optimistic What If possibilities we should consider.

What If La Perouse had decided they needed to build a stockade, like he had at Botany Bay, and to shoot at any local people who came to try and talk to them? What If, when he established the settlement of New New France, he started out with the mistrust of the locals?

Or What If the French started out with good intentions of friendly relations, but the locals caught diseases from them, and soon there were no First Nations people to oppose them building their settlement?

So any or all of those things could have happened, but regardless of which path we choose, the French soon had a settlement built on the land of New New France, named Louisville, with aspirations of it becoming a Paris of the south.

Place and faces

Now you'll pick this up as the story goes on, but if you are an explorer it is always considered wise to name lots of things after your bosses or whoever is paying for your expedition. After that you can name things after your family and friends (regardless of the fact that the people who lived there already had names for the places). For instance:

Van Diemen's Land was named by the Dutch explorer Abel Tasman after Anthony Van Diemen, the Governor-General of the Dutch East Indies who had funded his expedition.

Sydney Cove was named after Lord Sydney, the British Secretary of State for the Home Office, who made the decision to send convicts to Botany Bay.

Brisbane was named after Sir Thomas Brisbane the Governor of New South Wales at the time – and replaced the earlier name of Edenglassie (a combination of the Scottish cities Edinburgh and Glasgow).

Hobart was named after Robert Hobart, the Secretary of State for the Colonies at the time.

Victoria was named after Queen Victoria.

Melbourne was named after the British Prime Minister, William Lamb the 2nd Viscount Melbourne. It replaced the name Batmania, that was preferred by the founder of the settlement – John Batman!

CHAPTER 16

The Terror

Regardless of which What If path we travel along, there are soon more and more settlers arriving in New New France, putting pressure on the availability of land, which in turn puts pressure on good relations with the locals. And as the settlers spread out across the land, and try to understand its peculiarities and strange plants and animals, they give French names to things as they discover them.

French names of Australian animals:

Kangaroo	étrange houblon	(strange hoppy thing)
Wombat	fesses joufflus	(chubby bum animal)
Possum	yeux effrayants	(scary eyes)
Dingo	chien hostile	(unfriendly dog)
Koala	mignon mais sent la pisse	(cute but smells of pee)
Platypus	un quelle?	(a what?)
Kookaburra	oiseau drôle	(funny bird)

French names for Australian plants:

Wattle	fleur d'allergie	(allergy flower)
Banksia	essuie-glace de fond	(scratchy bottom wiper)
Waratah	ne pas manger	(do not eat)

And the key reason more and more settlers are arriving is that over in France things are getting a bit chaotic. Even before La Perouse had arrived back in France after dropping off the first French settlers, the French Revolution had started in July 1789.

The Revolution began because the peasants were sick of the way the nobles were not sharing their wealth, and many of them were starving, and so rose up against the rich. And since La Perouse was himself a noble that put a scare into him. His actual name and title was Jean François de Galaup, comte de Lapérouse. In plain speak he was the Count of La Perouse.

So when he gets back to France and finds everything in turmoil and the peasants overthrowing the nobility left and right, he says, 'Mon Dieu! The Peasants are revolting!'

And the other nobles say, 'Oui. They really are very terrible.'

Sorry – bad history joke.

So La Perouse offers to take lots of the nobles to New New France. They jump at the chance to escape the Revolution, and they load up several ships with all their money and useful things like gold nail clippers and expensive wigs and set off for the Southern Hemisphere – arriving sometime in 1790.

The nobles aren't very impressed with the small settlement, however, which isn't really what they were used to, and the settlers are less impressed with them and their reluctance to do any hard work. And the nobles also aren't too impressed with the reality of their ideas of Noble Savages. After all, in their minds they are the only ones who are allowed to be called noble!

They tell La Perouse, 'We expected something a little more grand. Something a little more like Paris.'

And he says, 'You are welcome to go back to Paris and face the angry peasants there.'

And they say, 'Well it's not that bad here. We'll see how we go.'

Now here's a very important question. If you were setting up a settlement in a new land, what type of people would you choose to have settle there? And if I gave you a choice between farming families who were used to working the land, and nobility who had never worked a day in their life, but had plenty of money – which would you choose?

If you went for the nobility and their money I'm sorry you would not be backing a winning choice. History is against you on that one. I mean the nobles started flashing their money around, of course, demanding new houses be built and new gardens be planted. But in a new colony money isn't actually worth very much. You can't eat money and you can't spend it if there is nothing really to buy.

But the nobles do have something of use. They have servants. Lots and lots of servants. Admittedly most are butlers and maids who are only skilled at serving them tea and wiping their bottoms after going to the toilet, but they are also pretty useful when being told to build things and clear land.

And that's what they do.

So while in the real Sydney Cove much of the work was done by convicts, here in our What If New New France it is being done by servants. It might not sound like a big difference, but it is pretty significant, as one set are prisoners and the other are free people. You don't need soldiers to guard free people and you don't need to chain them up and lie awake at nights fearful that they are going to escape and come and get you.

Though if you're digging a toilet ditch for your master you might not actually appreciate the difference, I guess.

CHAPTER 16

So the colony grows and the servants build bigger houses and roads and so on, and wait for news from home, hoping to hear that the Revolution has been overturned by the King of France and his armies.

But when news does finally come it isn't very good news. The revolutionaries are still in power, and France is now going through a really crazy time that becomes known as The Terror. This was when the craziest of the revolutionaries started executing the rich. You've seen pictures of a guillotine? It was named after a doctor, Joseph-Ignace Guillotin, who said it would permanently cure you of a headache.

Sorry, another bad history joke.

The Terror was a bad period for everyone – France was being attacked by its enemies, the Revolutionary Government was in crisis, and then what often happened during bad times happened. An absolute crazy person took control. In this instance he was Maximilien Robespierre.

If you look at his pictures you'll see he looks a bit like that try-hard kid in the class who is always smiling when the teacher is looking at him, but then he steals your lunch and smashes up your toys when no one is watching.

Robespierre

Under his rule thousands of people were executed for not being revolutionary enough, or for being a part of the aristocracy, or for telling jokes about him on TV. Okay, not that last one. I got confused with a few current political leaders.

Anyway, during the Terror even members of Robespierre's own political group who thought he was going too far were executed. The guillotines were running like a production line in a sliced sausage factory to keep up with numbers of people they had to execute. People were being encouraged to tell if they heard any citizens being disloyal to the revolution and that person would be hauled off to the guillotine. A good way to get rid of noisy neighbours who hadn't actually done anything wrong!

Even nuns were executed for not renouncing their faith, and one of the slogans of the nutty ruling group – the Committee for Public Safety was, for the Revolution to live the King must die!

Some historians have argued that Robespierre was just one of many political leaders driving the Terror, and he was not even the worst of them, but he became its public face. And it was not until he was overthrown and executed himself that the Terror finally came to an end, in July 1794.

Well, the nobles in New New France are of course terrified to hear about the Terror, and those few that have been considering going back to France quickly change their minds. But the servants, who are doing all the hard work as well as serving tea and wiping bottoms, start thinking that they might be better off if they have their own mini revolution, just like back home in France.

They take to the streets and shout slogans and wave French loaves at their masters and say they are not happy with the way things are being run.

The nobles don't quite know what to do about this, of course, and it looks like things are going to get very ugly, when something very unexpected happens. King Louis the 16th of France shows up in New New France.

He has managed to escape France, dressed as an old woman in a coach, with his wife Marie Antoinette. Accompanied by many of the Lords and Ladies of Court, the King has hired ships to take them to the only place he feels they can be safe and he can still be a King of France. New New France!

CHAPTER 16

Marie Antoinette: the truer facts

Born in Austria, 1755.

Died in France, 1793 (age 37).

Marie Antoinette's actual name was Maria Antonia Josepha Johanna, and she was an Archduchess of Austria. She was a good example of the belief that you don't need to be too clever if you are pretty.

She married the heir to the French throne in 1770, at the age of 15, and became Queen of France when he became King in 1774, four years later.

Despite her initial popularity with the French people, she slowly became a symbol of royal excess and of the blocking of social and financial reforms. As an example, she had an Austrian village built where she could pretend she was an Austrian peasant in a rural setting This was seen as a sign of her supporting Austria over France.

As the French Revolution began she was active in trying to prevent it, including seeking to crush the Revolution with Swiss mercenary troops. This was said to be one of the actions that triggered the storming of the Bastille jail – the popular start of the French Revolution.

She was later charged with sending French money to their enemies in Austria, and actively opposing the Revolution, and was executed by guillotine.

There is no real evidence that when told the French peasants had no bread to eat she said, 'Let them eat cake!' This was really a bit of less-true history invented by those who wanted people to think worse of her.

CHAPTER 17

Another Louis

Well the nobles at New New France now have something they haven't expected to have. A King.

And if you want to know what type of a King he was, he was actually considered a bit dim, and not really understanding what was going on about him. He was very unpopular amongst the people of France and was seen as treating the poor appallingly. If you look at his portrait you will see he was a little podgy with a sloping forehead that makes you think he only had an economy-sized brain in there. All in all, he was a bit dim and treated the poor appallingly.

Though to be fair, he was not quite as bad a King as his predecessor, Louis the 15th, who really was a terrible monarch. The King one before him, Louis the 14th, was very popular and was known as the Sun King, but his great grandson, Louis the 15th got involved in too many wars, spent too much money on his palace, and largely neglected the state of the people.

CHAPTER 17

King Louis XIV

King Louis XV

King Louis XVI

Then along came Louis the 16th, who was actually the grandson of Louis the 15th, and he had clearly learned too much from his grandfather. Including having the same name yet again. I mean, parents, really! Show some imagination please!

Can you picture the scene? Louis the some-random-number has just had a son and is jumping around the room in delight while his wife struggles to recover from the effort of pushing the little kid out.

'What will we call him do you think?' the King asks, having the nurse turn the baby this way and that to get a better view of him from different angles and to see what type of name might fit him.

'I had thought we might call him Jacque, after my father,' the Queen says, waiting for the nurse to hand the baby back so she can actually get to hold him.

'What's that you say?' asks the King. 'Louis?'

'No. I said Jacque. Anything but Louis. There are too many Louis' in your family already.'

'Yes, Louis is a very good name,' the King says. 'He does look a lot like a Louis, doesn't he?'

'You should have been called Loony, not Louis. I want to call him Jacque!'

'Louis it is then. What a grand choice of name.'

CHAPTER 17

Louis the 16th – or Louis the Little Bit Dim Who Ran Away to New New France – had a few personality faults, and his biggest was that he didn't think for himself often enough. Instead he tended to agree with whatever the last person he had spoken to had told him. And he really had a lot of rubbish advisers around, telling him things that weren't very sensible. Like how to treat the French people who were hungry and angry and fed up with big fat rich Kings living like – well Kings.

He learned that lesson the hard way, and in our What If history the only clever decision he makes on his own is to leave his rubbish advisers in France when he runs away. So here he is in New New France, worrying that the common people might be just as hungry and as angry and as interested in revolution as they are in France.

What's in a name?

When it comes to names parents clearly don't always think these things through well enough. For instance there was an American baseball player named Ten Million, and the musician Frank Zappa called his daughter Moon Unit Zappa. Also, the mutineer from the British ship the *Bounty*, Fletcher Christian, named his son Thursday October Christian. Yes, he was born on a Thursday in October, of 1790.

Maybe a little less imagination is sometimes called for!

But when it comes to strange names, royals tend to take the cake (what is it about royals and cake? – see box on Marie Antoinette). And if their names lacked variety, they sometimes made up of that in the strange official titles they were given. Here are a few you wouldn't want to have written on your school lunch box:

- Albert the Peculiar was a Duke of Austria in the late 14th century.
- Albert with the Pigtail was his father.
- Alexander the Potbelly was a Russian Prince in the 15th century.

- Alfonso the Slobberer was King of a part of ancient Turkey in the 12th century.
- Archibald the Grim and his son Archibald the Loser, of Scotland.
- Bernard the Hairy-Footed from France.
- Cadafael the Battle-Decliner, the Welsh King.
- Or the Holy Roman Emperor Charles the Fat.

My favourite two, for different reasons, are Colonom the Book-Lover of Hungary and Childeric the Idiot of France. Clearly they wouldn't have gotten on together at school.

Even all those Kings named Louis from France had their fair share of odd titles to distinguish them. Louis the 2nd was known as Louis the Stammerer, Louis the 4th was known as Louis the Foreigner, and Louis the 5th was known as Louis the Do-Nothing. Louis the 6th was Louis the Fat, followed by Louis the Young, and Louis the 10th was Louis the Stubborn.

So on the King's advice the French nobles start paying their servants more money to keep them happy (another idea of his own). And the nobles have lots and lots of money. So the servants start getting richer and richer themselves and suddenly the colony has an economy. Lots of people with enough money to buy things. Not much to buy, yet, but they could at least imagine it in their minds.

Now here's a thing about having lots of money and nothing to buy – people tend to find out and show up and offer to sell you all kinds of useless things. Pretty soon ships are stopping in New New France from India and Indonesia and Europe and Africa and selling their goods at greatly inflated prices to the French settlers – nobles and servants both.

The French are happy to be getting things to buy with their money at last, the merchants from all over are happy to be selling their goods at high prices and everyone is happy.

Well, not quite everyone. The local indigenous people are a bit worried at the pace the French colony is growing. With all these new things to buy servants work harder and harder building houses and roads and sewers and all kinds of things to earn more money to buy more stuff. And the more stuff they have the more the city grew. And the more it grew the more it expanded and took more land. And the more land it took the less land there is for the First Australians.

It reached a point where some of the local leaders ask to meet with the French King, and tell him their grievances.

CHAPTER 18

Meeting the neighbours

And here we could do a What If John Batman snuck back into the story and had become advisor to the King. Sort of like getting rid of some rubbish French advisors and replacing them with a rubbish English advisor. Or we could just have the French equivalent of him, Monsieur Homme Chauve-souris.[9]

He could have written his treaty document for the French and by signing it the local people got a couple of hundred berets and French loaves, and in exchange the French got most of their land.

So picture the scene. Half a dozen Elders are led in to see the King, and they come bearing green leaves of peace and wearing their best red berets, to complain about the way they have been tricked out of their land.

But when the King sees them he panics. He knows the French Revolutionaries had adopted a red cap as a

9 Yes, French for Mr Batman.

symbol of the Revolution, and he presumes the local people have come to overthrow him all over again, and his hides behind his throne.

His servants finally convince him that these aren't revolutionaries, and he climbs back onto his throne. One of his servants passes him a green branch that the locals have offered, and the King whispers, 'What is it for? Swatting away flies?'

'I believe it is a peace gesture,' says the servant.

'I thank you for your – um – gift,' says Louis, and throws it over his head behind the throne. He is much more used to giving jewels and things.

One of the Elders then steps forward and starts to outline their complaints, but Louis is looking at the Elder's possum skin cloak and thinking it is nowhere near as nice as the white fox furs on his own cloak.

Then he wonders what the Elders in front of him might look like if they were wearing wigs and had powdered faces. Then he notices they are not wearing pants and it makes him recall that dream he often has, of going to school with no pants on.

And all the while the Elders are talking to him and noticing that he not really listening. They stop talking and he looks at them eventually and says, 'Pardon? Could you say that all again?'

Needless to say the Elders are not particularly impressed with the King, and they go away grumbling about him, telling their friends and family that he should be known to them as Louis the Fat and Stupid.

And that evening Louis tells his wife, Marie Antoinette, 'I had the most fascinating meeting with some of the noble savages today.'

'Were they really noble?'

'Not as noble as us, of course.'

'What did they want?'

'I have no idea.'

Well, Louis might have thought that things in New New France were working out the best they could, and he was eagerly awaiting each new ship that arrived to see if it brought news of the Revolution having ended. But something very unexpected was happening in France.

A young Corsican General had taken over the French army. His name? Napoleon Bonaparte.

And yes, you might think that was a pretty strange name to give a person, and he probably got teased a lot at school for it. But that might well be the reason he was so driven to become a famous general and take over the world – to make all those kids who teased him regret it.

In fact, every time Napoleon conquered a new country he'd have a statue of himself made – a little bigger each time – and have it sent back to his school (and all of the statues had pants on). At least in our What If history he does.

What drives famous people?[10]

And here's a thing about the men and women who go on to do great things in history, and become really famous, that you won't find on Wikipedia. Most of them were driven to succeed because they were teased at school. (And the other ones were mostly trying really hard to impress a girl or a guy). Here's a list of some of them:

- Queen Elizabeth the First: teased by her half sister Mary.
- Julius Caesar: wanted to impress Cleopatra.
- Mahatma Gandhi: teased at school.
- Christopher Columbus: wanted to impress a girl.
- Abraham Lincoln: teased at school.
- William Shakespeare: wanted to impress a girl.
- Albert Einstein: teased at school.
- Henry VIII: wanted to impress several girls.

10 No, the answer is not: Their Chauffeur.

170 cm

CHAPTER 19

Enter Napoleon

Anyway, you probably know a lot about Napoleon already, right? Like you'd know he was small, he has appeared in lots of TV shows, and he stuck one hand inside his shirt front.

Well, here are a few things you might not know about him.

Firstly, he wasn't actually small. That was something made up by the English to make fun of him. He was about 1.7 metres tall, which was pretty average for those days. However, for a big tough military leader, not given to showing any fear in battle, he was very afraid of cats.

Another fact about Napoleon that has been supported by many sources at the time was that despite being brilliant at many things, he was absolutely rubbish at singing. Also, his favourite thing in the world was licorice, which he just about always had on hand to eat and over time it stained his teeth a dark colour. You don't see that in the paintings though, because unlike photography, the painters had quite a bit of license in turning the looks in front of them into better-looking portraits. And if you wanted a good fee, you'd paint a good portrait. (And there was also a strong possibility that the painter might be punished if he actually painted the Emperor with black teeth!)

Anyway my favourite quirk of Napoleon was that he cheated at cards. He was so driven to win at everything, his aids commented that he would often cheat in order to win.

But despite those odd quirks, he did a lot of very amazing things and was as talented an administrator as he was a general. He thoroughly reformed French laws, making them more uniform and simpler. He also reformed schools and put a lot of emphasis on education (unless you were a female or had dark-coloured skin!). He stabilised the economy, set a fixed price for bread, started up a national lottery to raise money, and oddly enough he even started the idea of even house numbers on one side of the street and odd numbers on the other. (Oddly enough – get it?)

And every country he occupied he made it compulsory to travel on the right-hand side of the road. Traditionally people travelled on the left, so they could draw a sword in their right hand to fight off anybody threatening them. But Napoleon stopped that, and in Europe only Britain, that was never conquered by Napoleon, still drives on the left-hand side. True fact!

But something else of great importance to know, Napoleon and his wife Josephine were very interested in Australia.

Empress Josephine: The truer facts

Born in 1763.

Died in 1814, aged 50.

With the very impressive full name of Marie Josèphe Rose Tascher de La Pagerie, Josephine was married to a French nobleman, Alexandre de Beauharnais, at the age of 16. But the marriage was effectively over when she was 20. Just as well for her, as her husband was guillotined during the Terror period of the French Revolution. She herself was imprisoned during this period.

So she was a widow with two children, and was six years older than Napoleon, when he met her in 1795. He was 26 and she was 32 and he was smitten with her. and they married the next year. Two days after the wedding he marched off to war against Italy, but sent her continuous love letters.

If you look at her portraits you'll see she was very attractive, with dark hair, but you will also see there are many different variations of her looks in different portraits. So clearly she was rich and powerful enough (and married to Napoleon) so nobody was going to paint a bad picture of her.

The long separations put a strain on their marriage of course, and when she was unable to bear him a son, he argued they should divorce in the interests of France, so that he could have an heir to the empire. (Ironic considering he had a few illegitimate children!) Napoleon insisted Josephine retain the title of Empress though.

Napoleon then married Marie Louise of Austria in 1811 – whose full name was Maria Ludovica Leopoldina Franziska Therese Josepha Lucia (though he actually had a stand-in at the church to take the vows for him). He was 40 and she was 18. They had a son two years later, who became Napoleon II. Napoleon hoped he would take over his rule, but he died at the age of 21, while in exile.

However Napoleon III did rule France, providing great stability for the country. And ironically, he was Josephine's grandson. His parents were Napoleon's brother, Louis Bonaparte, and Josephine's daughter Hortense. Josephine was also great-grandmother of several Swedish and Danish Kings and Queens (yes it is complicated I know).

When Josephine died Napoleon was in exile on the island of Elba, having been defeated by a coalition of European armies, eating meals off plates with her image on them. He is said to have locked himself in his rooms for two days on hearing the news.

Peron

CHAPTER 20

Beating Napoleon at something

So now we have to go back to that crazy Frenchman Francois Peron – the one with the dynanometre device to measure strength – who wrote the report on how the French could invade and conquer the British Settlement at Port Jackson. Remember him? If you look up his picture you'll see he looked a bit like an evil scientist wearing a really silly hat, plotting to take over the world. Which wasn't too far from the reality of things.

He was both a doctor and a naturalist on the expedition of Nicolas Baudin. Though he clearly seemed to think he was also a spy.

The expedition left France in 1801 with 22 naturalists on board two ships. Compared to Cook's small handful of naturalists it was clearly an attempt by the French to prove they could do the science better than the English could.

The expedition was authorised by Napoleon to explore, to chart and then to claim Australia's southern coast and call it 'Terre Napoleon' (Napoleon Land – of course). Napoleon had a long interest in Australia, and if you recall when he was just 16, in 1785, he had tried to join La Perouse's expedition.

We've already asked that big What If question, as to what would have happened if he did join La Perouse and disappeared at sea too, and there was never a Napoleon in Europe. One of the big differences might be in the USA, as Napoleon sold a huge chunk of land across the middle of the United States that had been claimed by France, to the Americans to fund his war with Britain. The size of land was about a third of the current USA, and it was known as the Louisiana Purchase.

CHAPTER 20

Anyway, back to our main story about Francois Peron on the expedition that Napoleon sent out to do better than the British had done. The expedition's two ships, the *Géographe* and the *Naturaliste* reached Western Australia in May of 1801 and they mapped the coast there and also bits of the largely unexplored southern coast. Of course they left behind suitably French names such as Gulf Bonaparte and Gulf Josephine.

Then, after visiting Van Diemen's Land and Port Jackson, they sailed for home.

Unfortunately the expedition leader Nicolas Baudin died of tuberculosis at the island of Mauritius on the return voyage. So Peron took over. And the first thing he did was to cross Baudin's name out of the official account of the voyage.

Evil scientist wanting to take over the world, yes?

But the expedition did bring back thousands of botanical and zoological specimens – including kangaroos and emus. And many of these were given to Napoleon and his wife Josephine.

Her prized possessions were two black swans, but she also cultivated the seeds of many plants brought back. She had a large glasshouse and the first Australian plants grown were named after her – Josephinia Imperatrcicis. If I knew what type of plant that was, I'd describe it, but since I don't we'll just move on. Sorry plant lovers.

The next big thing that happened was that Napoleon, the victorious military leader and First Consul of the Republic of France, decided to make himself the Emperor of France. Which was a bit odd when you consider he had opposed the King.

Napoleon made himself Emperor of France in 1804 (so not an evil scientist, but still very interested in taking over the world). The problem we run into is that there were now two French leaders, both claiming to be the rightful ruler of France: Napoleon and Louis the 16th.

CHAPTER 20

While they were on different sides of the world, in our story, that was fine enough, but you just know they are going to end up in the same land arguing over who is the rightful leader, right?

Of course they will. And this is how it happens.

The Kings and Queens of Europe were aghast when Napoleon took over as leader of France, and proved himself as a bit of a military genius. This very, very minor noble was kicking their butts all across the continent. Something had to be done about him! Especially since it meant they might find themselves out of a job and replaced by people like him in their own countries.

But every time they sent an army up against him – he defeated them. And then he made himself Emperor! A man with no royal blood! This only increased fear and anger at him more.

Then, when Napoleon started sending scientific expeditions around the world – and claiming things for France – the British in particular got a bit worried. They had counted on Captain Cook claiming much of the land down south for England. But since in our What If story he never returned to England, they decided that if they didn't get a move on there wouldn't be much left to claim.

We could of course do some more What If-ing, and have a lone survivor of Captain Cook's voyage show up in England, having been rescued or made his way to

Dutch Batavia[11]. He could tell the authorities that Cook had claimed much of the coast and that would be enough for the British to stake a more permanent claim to it. So they put together some ships and send them down there to establish a settlement before the French expand their claim across more of the land.

I mean, they had to beat Napoleon at something, right!

And where do they end up? Sydney Cove, of course. Well, it is the obvious place for a settlement really. I mean Jervis Bay is pretty nice, and Bateman's Bay isn't too bad either, but if you're thinking of a place that is easy to defend against the French, the cliffs around Sydney Cove and the size of the harbour inside make Sydney Harbour a clear winner.

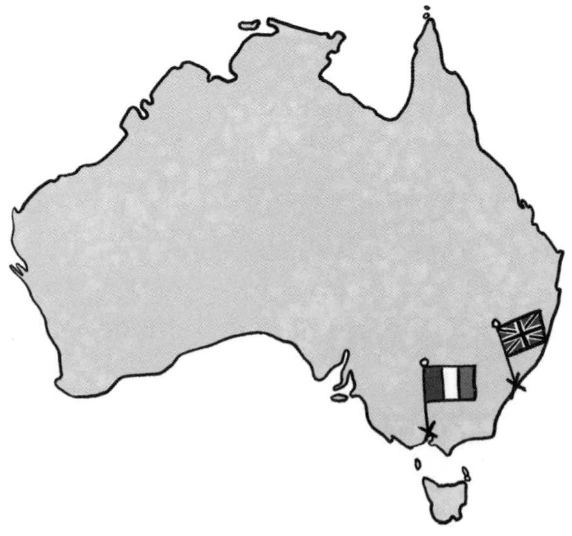

11 Present day Jakarta in Indonesia.

CHAPTER 21

Enter Governor Davey

So in the year 1810, 22 years after the real First Fleet arrived, the What If First Fleet arrives and sails into one of the most beautiful harbours in the world (if you live in Sydney). Or an over-rated and over-priced harbour full of sharks (if you live in Melbourne or anywhere else).

The man chosen to head the settlement is Thomas Davey, a former Captain in the British marines who had fought against Napoleon at the Battle of Trafalgar. To be honest he was a bit of an idiot, very self-obsessed, and drank far too much – but his father was very good at begging for favours on his behalf.

If you look at a picture of him you'll see he has that stunned look on his face like he has just been told he is a self-obsessed drunken idiot, or has been hit in the face with a stick. But he was a man in need of a job and those who he worked with in England clearly thought sending him to the far side of the globe was the perfect place to be.

Thomas Davey

CHAPTER 21

In real life, Thomas Davey became Lieutenant-Governor of Van Diemen's Land. He was famous for trying to sneak out of England without his wife and daughter, and then leaving them behind in Van Diemen's Land when he finally returned to England. And as Lieutenant-Governor he demonstrated himself to be a bit of a self-obsessed drunken idiot.

So in our What If history we have him leading a whole fleet of ships loaded with supplies for several years and soldiers and convicts. Lots of convicts. And if you want to know what it's like to be a convict on a ship at that time, being transported across the ocean, it's not much different to being a piece of cargo, I can tell you.

You are stuck below decks sleeping three or more to a bed space that isn't much better than a wooden platform that you might stack cargo on. And you get rubbish food lowered down to you in a bucket – if the weather is calm enough. And you get another bucket to poop and wee into, which gets lifted up on a rope and emptied – if the weather is calm enough. And you don't want to get those buckets mixed up, believe me.

And if one person gets sick you'll probably all catch it, and if you die they just haul you up and throw you over the side. And the journey lasts for weeks and weeks and weeks.

And how do I know this exactly? Well I know this because in researching this book I became a convict and was chained up in an old sailing ship that went from England to Australia. Well, that's actually a What If story. I didn't really do that. Though I did lie in the hammock in my backyard and think about it.

But you can imagine how the trip would have been. The fleet would have sailed around the Cape of Good Hope in South Africa and then headed straight on towards Western Australia, using the roaring forties trade winds to push them along.

CHAPTER 21

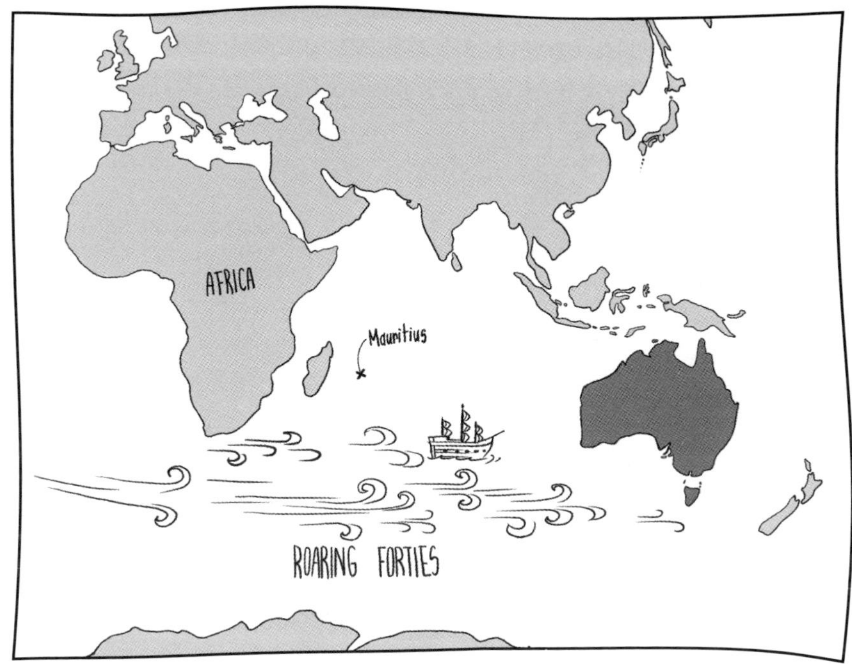

They would also be keeping a lookout for French ships, as the islands of Mauritius, east of Madagascar, were French territory – known as Isle de France. As such there was a lot of French shipping likely to be in that part of the Indian Ocean, and the What If First Fleet was keen to avoid them.

I mean it was one thing to send out all your best warships looking for a fight, but it was quite another to be in a fleet of mixed civilians and foot soldiers, loaded down with goods and cows and pigs and sheep and women and children and so on – and run into French warships. You couldn't just fire a pig or two at them.

So they are planning on stealth and relying on good fortune – which was a pretty bold thing to do in those days when there more ways of dying than you could poke a stick at (including dying from being poked by a stick!). And going to sea on a long voyage just increased the chances of some of those accidents or diseases or things catching you.

Anyway, they have planned to reach Western Australia, turn sharp left and follow the Dutch trading routes to the Spice Islands of Java, and then go over the top of Australia and down the eastern side to the proposed site of their settlement.

Here's how I imagine it. The captain of one ship that is a little slower than the others and struggling to keep up with the fleet is on deck, nervously pacing back and forth and looking at the ships ahead and the empty ocean behind him. Suddenly a man up in the rigging shouts, 'Sail to the port side!'

'Is she French?' the captain calls back.

'I think so,' the sailor calls.

'Quick,' the captain says to his second mate, 'Go and fetch my red shirt.'

'Of course sir, but why?'

'Well if that is a French ship and they engage in fire with us and I'm hit, I don't want the men to see blood on my shirt and become anxious.'

'Of course sir,' the man says. And he runs off and gets the captain's red shirt.

'I see more sails,' the man in the riggings suddenly calls out.

'How many more sails?' the captain calls to him.

'About twenty,' the sailor calls.

'Quick,' the captain says to the second mate. 'Go and fetch my brown trousers!' [12]

12 An old joke, but a good one, which in a What If history, nobody has ever heard before.

CHAPTER 22

New South Scotland

So when this What If First Fleet arrives at Sydney Cove, having escaped any French ships they encounter, and having avoided the dangers of the barrier reef by sailing around it, and having washed any brown trousers that needed cleaning, they look at the land and decide it looks a lot like southern Scotland.

So they call it New South Scotland.

Then they scout around the harbour for the best bit of land to settle on.

You can guess the conversation they had about that. The northern side of the shore looked a bit posh, the western side of the harbour looked a bit rough, but the southern side looked pretty good.

Governor Davey half-closed his eyes and imagined a city there one day that looked something like London, with a tower bridge over the harbour, ships going up and down the waterways, and something that looked like a cut open white fruit that might be some kind of a house for singing opera.

CHAPTER 22

So the Governor, the head of the marines and the other notables of the settlement are rowed ashore and they find a nice bit of flat land and stick in a British flag and proclaim the settlement of New London.

But of course when it is pointed out by one of the more worldly officers that there is already a New London in the Americas they update the name to New New London.

So there they are, bringing the settlers ashore and measuring out ground for where they'll put the cattle and the sheep and where the Governor's quarters will be built, and where the first farms will be, and where the soldier's barracks will go, and where they'll mount cannons to fire on any hostile ships that come into the harbour, and where they'll put the convicts who are going to build all this for them.

Governor Davey, having landed all his men and their livestock, orders everyone to start building a colony – but the land perplexes them. The many eucalyptus trees are as hard as rock and defy their axes, and none seem to grow straight enough to cut planks for building from. Also the leaves stay on the trees and the bark falls off! And then there are the native birds which are as bright as tropical fruit, but screech like creatures from your nightmares.

Even the ground defies their first attempts to plough and plant things. And of course the local people hide from them, or oppose their taking of their land.

But Governor Davey is not a man to give up easily. Mainly because that would have meant making a decision. He instructs all his men to just carry on, and make sure they build him a first-rate cottage with a bird bath. He does so like a nice bird bath.

So the convicts are building fortifications and mounting cannons and the soldiers chase away the local First Nations people and the settlers start clearing land for farms.

There are other differences with the real First Fleet too – which was basically a huge load of convicts and lots of soldiers to guard them. In our What If story the British want to establish both a military base and settlement, and so they actually sent some people who knew a little bit about farming and building and things, rather than those who just knew about stealing and forging (which you have to admit are fairly limited skills when it comes to establishing a new settlement in an unknown land).[13]

Having only soldiers and convicts they would have been considered a strategic military base and penal colony, but having a large number of free settlers supports the British claim to be establishing a proper settlement. And if the

13 Though stealing the land off the locals was a pre-requisite for any settlement on the continent!

French ever accuse them of military aggression, they could claim the soldiers were just there for protection, and the convicts were there as labour for the settlers. And for building nice bird baths, of course.

Military Base

Free Colony

Of course Governor Davey never thinks to ask permission of the locals to land there, or to even consider that somebody else might have any form of ownership of the land. Because if they did they would have built towns and things there, right? Villages at the very least. And all he could see were dark-skinned people skulking in the woods, who had at best a few huts built here and there.

They didn't even have any ornate bird baths!

So the logic of the time often went – if you didn't have signs of civilisation, then you didn't have civilised people. And if you didn't have civilised people, you had a right to civilise the land yourself, right!

Which history shows us was another mistaken and bad idea.

CHAPTER 23

If you didn't have any signs of civilisation...

But What If we consider things from a different perspective once more?

Imagine modern day Sydney, in all its glass and glistening splendor[14], and suddenly an alien spaceship descends over the city. It is huge and is full of colonists looking for a new land to settle. And imagine these aliens look something like us, but are much, much more advanced, to the point that they respect and value the natural environment above all else and they look at Sydney and think – OMG what primitive peoples! Look at the lack of natural spaces. Look at all the concrete and glass and bitumen and crowds! Look at all the rubbish they are generating and the noise and the pollution!

And they decide Sydney will be an excellent place for a settlement, particularly the bits of land overlooking the

14 Yes, yes, and with lots of traffic jams and smog and rush hour crowds.

harbour. They just need to clear away all those horrible buildings to do it. I mean, surely, if these primitive people actually valued the land here they'd leave it pristine, or they would live with it in a more environmentally-friendly way.

I mean, if you don't have any signs of civilisation, then you don't have civilised people. And if you don't have civilised people, you have a right to civilise the land yourself, right!

How would you feel about that? Especially if it was your house that they flattened to regrow trees and grassland and so on, on top of?

Do you really think you'd say, 'Well that's okay. Go ahead and smash up our city and take our land and build whatever you need to build on top of it. We don't mind that you never asked us about it, and why should you, because you are clearly a more advanced civilisation?'

I'm guessing probably no. And that is pretty much what the local Gadigal people thought too. But what would you do if you were facing alien beings with powerful death rays that also carried lots of diseases that you had no immunity to? You might move further away, you might try and make friends, or you might get angry. Really angry!

In real life a Bidgigal man named Pemulwuy led resistance against the British settlers for many years around Sydney, stealing food and attacking settlers. But in our What If version of history, What If a similar warrior, a generation later, such as Pemulwuy's son Tedbury, started leading resistance raids against the British?

In some ways it might have been harder as there are more military men in our What If First Fleet. But there would also be a lot more flocks of sheep and cows to steal as well. And more farmlands to steal crops from.

The guerilla war between the settlers and the First Nations people could last a long, long time, and it might be dependent on the military being able to engage in a war with the locals, or have to engage in a war with the French.

And what do you think is going to happen next in our story?

Of course the French are going to go to war with the British. But we'll get to that by and by.

Pemulway: The truer facts

Born about 1750.

Died in 1802, about 52 years old.

Pemulwuy was born nearby Botany Bay and was described as having a blemish in one eye and one foot was a little deformed. While there had been earlier small incidents of the locals attacking settlers, Pemulwuy led a much more concerted resistance. He first came to notice when he speared a settler in 1790 – the Governor's gamekeeper.

After that he led raids on settlers at Prospect, Toongabbie, George's River, Parramatta, Brickfield Hill and at the Hawkesbury River. He was described by David Collins, the Secretary to the Governor, as: "a most active enemy to the settlers, plundering them of their property, and endangering their personal safety".

Military parties were sent out to hunt Pemulwuy, but it was a civilian party that finally cornered him. He was wounded by buckshot to his head and body, and was taken to the nearby hospital but escaped and recovered from his wounds in the bush.

In 1801, Governor King issued a proclamation that any Aborigines near Parramatta, Georges River or Prospect could be shot on sight. Later than year Pemulwuy was proclaimed an outlaw with a reward offered for his capture.

That reward was claimed by one Henry Hacking, who shot him dead in 1802. The story goes that his head was then cut off and sent to England, though no record of that has ever been verified.

He was described both as have been a terrible nuisance to the colony, but also as being a brave and independent resistance fighter.

Showing that depending who writes the history, you can often be many things.

CHAPTER 24

What If we had a different Governor?

There is another What If we could look at in regard to our What If First Fleet. What If the British had sent a different Governor to New South Scotland who was more like Governor Arthur Phillip? Unlike our Governor Davey, Governor Phillip tried very hard to establish good relations with the locals (well apart from stealing their land and allowing his soldiers to shoot at them when they felt threatened).

Governor Phillip named the northern beaches area of Sydney Manly because he felt the locals there were very manly. And he had a leading start over many of his own men in trying to engage with the locals, because he had a missing front tooth – and an initiation practice amongst the locals was to knock out a front tooth! True fact!

Governor Arthur Phillip

He also passed a decree that there be no slavery in the new colony, 20 years before slavery was banned in Britain. Overall, for his time, he was a pretty okay guy. Certainly better than some of the lazy or self-interested governors that followed him in real life.

Or What If the British Government had authorised the Governor to negotiate a treaty with the locals? What If there was a legal document that stated their rights and gave them some legal status within the new colony? What If it was a part of the Governor's orders that he had to learn the local languages and customs, not because he had a personal interest in it, but because it was the way his superiors wanted the colony to be built?

But yeah, having an alien spacecraft land in Sydney and level all the houses and buildings was probably more likely to happen!

CHAPTER 25

King Louis the 16th arrives at New New France

So we have the British busy at New New London establishing farms and things and building roads and little pubs that serve warm beer and potato crisps. And we have the French in New New Paris busy building large ornate buildings and monuments to the exiled King, and baking French loaves. Both are trying very, very hard to prove they have the best colony – mirroring not only the rivalry between France and England, but that between Sydney and Melbourne.

Of course there is a bit of a gap between the expectations of the French and British and what they are actually building. For instance, in France the King had a giant and luxurious palace at Versailles. You might have heard of it. It was so palatial that people were known to have gone in there to deliver a message and never come out again, having got lost in the many rooms and corridors.

Okay, I made that bit up. But it was certainly very big with over 700 rooms. It had about everything a palace could need – except for sufficient running water and working toilets. There wasn't enough water at Versailles for everything you needed water for – like did I mention toilets?

King Louis the 14th, who had it built, wanted lots of water fountains around the grounds to impress visitors. But the only way to make them work when some foreign dignitary came to visit was to have a small army of gardeners running around behind the hedges, switching fountains off that the dignitaries had just walked past, and switching those on that they were now walking up to.

Anyway – the point of that story is that while King Louis the 16th wanted a palace as grand as Versailles built for him in New New France, there is no way that was going to happen. He is lucky to get a large brick building painted a yellow colour that at sunset, if you squeeze your eyes half-shut, looks just a little bit like gold.

The rooms inside his brick house are not quite as palatial as those at Versailles either, but the King goes to great trouble to pretend to himself that they are. He even has some backdrops painted that make it look like there is a grand ballroom or something there, where in fact it is just a wall.

You can imagine the What If scene of him arriving in New New France and his ship sailing into the bay and making its way across the waters towards where they can see smoke arising. The King has been told of the colony, and expects to see something at least a little bit like France – constructed in just a few short years.

But as the ship gets closer, all he can see are tents and huts. There are a few more substantial brick buildings, but not very many. When you are establishing a new colony building places to live is important, of course, but not quite as important as having food and water, and so growing crops was getting a higher priority than building houses.

If you ever study sociology or psychology there is a thing called Maslow's hierarchy of needs. It was developed by a psychologist named Abraham Maslow. It is a very useful thing to know. Draw a pyramid (without any Ancient Egyptians in the picture) and then you write your most important needs at the bottom of it. And as you go up you write your next most important needs and so on, until you have less important things at the top. So those most important things at the bottom tend to be food and water and sleep and breathing and so on. Then you move up to things like shelter and security, and then keep on going up until they reach things like ability to take a selfie, and clean underpants and free wi-fi (which some people, I know, might prefer to place right down the bottom as the most important of needs – but go and talk to Abraham Maslow about it).

Anyway, the point is that King Louis the 16th clearly had a slightly different hierarchy of needs than most of the other settlers.

But back to the day the King arrives at the settlement. Picture a beautiful cloudy and dim typical Melbourne day, and King Louis the 16th comes ashore with some upper-class army officers who have proclaimed themselves his personal guard. They are met by a settler who is, of course, very surprised to find the King of France standing there. He tells the King, 'Your Majesty, I am very honoured that you have come to visit us.'

The King looks past him, like he is expecting someone else.

The man then says, 'I hope your Majesty will like what he sees of our settlement.'

The King looks at him and says, 'Yes. But where is it?'

'It is here,' the man says, gesturing at the tents and huts and the small crowd that is now assembling. Then the man is bold enough to ask, 'By chance are your ships carrying any gifts of supplies for your loyal subjects? Like bottles of wine or French cheese or something nice like that?'

The King does not quite know how to answer that, and so leaves it to one of his army officers to tactfully explain that the King is not here to visit – but he is coming here to live. He then explains that the situation in France has gotten just a little bit crazy. He leaves out telling him that it is so crazy in fact that if they caught the King they would execute him.

The King then says, 'Call me a coach to take me to the palace.'

But the settler says, 'I'm sorry, we don't have any coaches.'

The King looks a little annoyed but says, 'Then we shall have to ride. Have our horses brought up and show us the road to the palace.'

'Uh – we don't really have any roads either,' the settler says.

'So how does one reach the palace?' the King asks.

The settler seems really pained by this question and grits his teeth as if trying not to let the answer out, but finally says, 'Uh – we don't actually have any palaces here. At least not yet.'

CHAPTER 25

The King stares at him in horror. Aghast. His wife, Marie Antoinette, who has now come up beside him with her ladies in waiting, whispers in his ear that they should have the horrid little man sent off to one of Frances's far-flung colonies. 'But we are in one of France's far-flung colonies, *mon chérie*[15],' he tells her.

The nobles and army officers then have a quick conference with the settlers and they buy the biggest and best building that exists – a brick building that has, until this day, been their schoolhouse.

It is now going to be their palace.

'Do you remember, your Excellency,' one officer comes back to tell the King, 'When the palace of Versailles was once just a hunting lodge?'

'That was long before my time,' the King says, 'but yes I remember the stories.'

'Well imagine you are Louis the 14th going to your hunting lodge,' the officer says.

And if there is something that our Louis the 16th really likes, it is imagining that he's Louis the 14th. After all, he was popular. He was known as the Sun King. He had money and influence. And the peasants thought he was mostly a good sort, and did not want to revolt and overthrow him.

15 My dear. Honey pie. Main squeeze.

'Come then,' he tells Marie Antoinette. 'It will be quite an adventure.'

So King Louis moves into his palace and spends most of his days sitting on an uncomfortable wooden chair (that was just a little bit higher than any other chair in the room), in the largest room of his brick house that he imagines is going to be just as grand as Versailles.

One day.

And Marie Antoinette has laid out an assortment of hand mirrors so it is almost as ornate as the vast hall of mirrors in Versailles.

Almost.

But our King Louis is clearly a man who could imagine things to be other than they were. Like he imagines that he is going to get invited back to France to become King again. Like he imagines he is Louis the 14th, the Sun King, and popular with everyone. And like he imagines that he has some ability to turn himself invisible and go into the kitchen and steal as many cakes as he likes without his wife knowing, but instead gets lectured about how he sits down all day and eats too many cakes and is getting too fat and needs to get out more.

Marie Antoinette saying to a cook, with a cake on the bench, 'Don't let him eat cake.' King Louis peeping into the kitchen around the door in the background.

And he tells her that a writer has to sit down to write. Sorry – I meant a king has to sit down to do king things. This is definitely not a reference to somebody who might be writing a book about What If histories. This is about being a king in a What If history.

Just to make that clear.

CHAPTER 26

Meanwhile, back in France...

So back to Europe, where events in real life continued to have an impact on Australia. Napoleon, that great military genius, finally did something that wasn't so great and wasn't so genius. He tried to invade Russia! That proved to be something so dumb that Louis the 15th or 16th might have attempted it.

The problem was that Russia was a long, long, long way away from France and had really, really, really cold winters. So by the time Napoleon reached the Russian capital Moscow, in 1812, it was winter and his army were tired and worn out and hungry and lots of them were sick, and not well prepared for the winter cold.

The Russians, who Napoleon had kept defeating, had kept retreating as he advanced, burning the land as they went so that there was nothing for the French troops to steal or eat. And they kept retreating until they were somewhere on the far side of Moscow, waiting for the obvious to happen. Well, it was obvious to them, but not so much to Napoleon it seems.

Winter arrived!

Then to make things worse for Napoleon fires broke out all over the city and pretty much burned Moscow down.

Napoleon blamed Russian spies and the Russians blamed careless French troops for the fires. But either way, for a short time there were lots of fires to cook on and keep warm by. Unfortunately they didn't actually have much to cook, and when the fires died out they had nowhere to seek shelter.

So there was nothing for it but to claim they had beaten the Russian army, yet were defeated by the Russian winter, and to turn around and march back to France.

Now here's another thing about warfare back then that it is important to know. When you moved a large army anywhere they would live off the land – which meant stealing everything possible to eat as they went. Which was all well and good unless you had to turn around and go back the way you had come. Because then you'd find that you had already stolen and eaten pretty much everything worth eating and stealing. And worse if the army you had been chasing had burned the land you had to trek through, there was even less than pretty much nothing.

So there was Napoleon's army, miserably trying to trek back to France in the snow, with nothing much to eat, and the soldiers developing diseases like typhus, and being chased by Russian soldiers who were more used to the cold. And then the armies of just about every other European country who Napoleon had already beaten, joined in too, intent on revenge.

And let me tell you a little bit about marching across Europe in the chill of winter. The word cold doesn't even begin to describe it. Imagine the coldest you've ever been and then multiple it by about 20. It is so cold that you find your whole body is shivering like it is going to shake apart. Your fingers and toes are so cold that you can't feel them, and they even start to hurt like they have been burned.

CHAPTER 26

And you find your body stops working like it should. You have trouble concentrating on where you are going and trouble remembering things, and all you can think about is being warm.

And how do I know this exactly? Well I know this because in researching this book I walked from Russia to France in the winter, wearing the types of clothes they wore in Napoleon's army.

And do you know what else? Yes, that's actually another What If dodgy truth.

But I did walk down to the shops in my thongs on a really cold day!

CHAPTER 27

New New France welcomes a new ruler

Napoleon, and what was left of his army, reached Paris in 1814, to find that the leaders of Paris had already surrendered and they had passed an Act to have him declared deposed, to save the enemy armies from invading the city.

Napoleon wasn't very happy about this, but his generals also refused to keep fighting, and also pressed him to step down.

The victorious forces at first wanted to exile him to somewhere in the Mediterranean Sea, like the small island of Elba – which is what happened in real life. But some wise person pointed out that he might just escape, return to France, raise an army all over again and have to be beaten once more, with combined European forces fighting him at a place like, say, Waterloo – which would in turn become a best-selling hit for the cheesy Swedish pop group Abba.

So in our story, to avoid such a song ever being written the rulers of Europe decided to exile Napoleon to New New France.

And so, in 1815 he arrives there with a large following of loyal servants and soldiers.

King Louis the 16th is by now an old man of 61, and is perhaps looking forward to a peaceful retirement in exile, enjoying his collection of ornate clocks – so he is about as displeased to see Napoleon arrive as the rulers of Europe are pleased to see him gone.

Napoleon was a little anxious about the type of place he'd be going to. He'd read some of the reports about New New France, saying the weather was very pleasant and the land fertile and easy to farm, promising great prosperity. And he has also heard that there was gold scattered around on the ground, and precious gems could be found in the soil. But he has long ago dismissed these reports as clumsy royalist propaganda to attract settlers. So he asks his British guards who are escorting him to the bottom of the world to tell him what they know of New New France.

Unfortunately they only have British propaganda to go on, and so tell him what they know. 'I have heard it is a devilish place. There are godless natives that will kill you in your sleep and eat your fingers and drink your blood.'

'I have heard that there are snakes that are so large they can swallow a man whole. And they are poisonous too.'

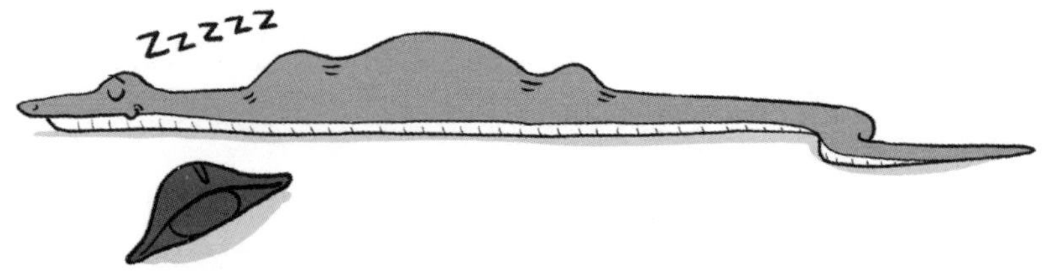

'I read that it is so hot that you can bake a French loaf on the ground.'

'A French friend of my wife's Belgian cousin visited there, and he said that the water is foul, the plants are all poisonous and the animals are all dangerous.'

'Yes! They have bears. Small but very vicious. And they lurk in the trees and drop down on top of you if you walk underneath.'

So Napoleon is pleasantly surprised to find that when he eventually reaches New New France it is not like either the French nor British reports. But he is disappointed in the lack of a welcoming contingent of loyal citizens waiting for him, waving the French tricolor and proclaiming him their Emperor. Though it would have been very surprising if that had happened, not just because no one knew he was coming, but because most of the settlers are royalists who opposed him.

Just as well he has brought his own fan squad of 1,000 of the Imperial Guard and several ministers and senior officials from his administration that the new French Government had sent into exile with him. So Napoleon has them line up on the shore and cheer him as he walks down the gangplank of his ship, with his wife Marie Louise on one arm, and his former wife Josephine on the other.

You can imagine him walking around and shaking hands with his men, who tell him how pleased they are to see him. And Napoleon thinks this is going to work out splendidly. Until he has some of his soldiers go and find one of the settlers to tell him where his palace is.

And you know how this conversation goes.

CHAPTER 27

So again there is a muttered discussion between some officers and a settler and again some money changes hands and again he is led off to a small, yellow-painted brick building.

It is big by the settlement's standards – but to Napoleon it is about the same size as his gatekeeper's cottage. But he is a man of great vision.

'This will do splendidly for a start,' he says to his nervous officers. 'We will have extensions made. And then we shall extend on those extensions.'

Napoleon is ushered into the house, through the front door and is pleased to see many servants there. Even if they do look confused to see him. 'Bon jour,' he says to each as he passes.

The entrance is well decorated, he thinks. Some very fine furniture and nice tapestries and paintings on the walls. The people are to be congratulated for getting this ready for him.

But then he walks into the main room and sees King Louis the 16th sitting there on a slightly raised chair, staring at him like he had just seen a vicious bear drop from a tree and land on his wife's head.

Now in normal circumstances the King might have even seen Napoleon and his entourage coming, except that he had one of his servants paint pictures to hang outside the windows that looked like the gardens of the palace of Versailles. Or it would have looked like the gardens if he'd chosen a servant who had the slightest idea about painting. So outside the windows actually looked more like an African jungle with weird statues in it.

Anyway, one of the King's servants had just knocked on the door to warn him, breaking his train of thought about where he might find a better artist in the colony. He looks up and a man pushes past the servant and stares at him.

'Um – announcing the Emperor of France, Napoleon Bonaparte,' the servant says.

Now the King gets over his surprise quickly and thinks this a great joke, sending someone in to impersonate Napoleon. His family constantly make jokes about him, like, 'What is Boney short for?' – 'It's because he has little legs!'

Yeah, okay the joke works better when you ask *What is ET short for?* – but you get the idea.[16]

So Napoleon strides into the room and the King starts clapping his hands. 'Oh spectacular,' he says. 'You look just like him! But they should have found someone shorter I think.'

Napoleon glares at him and says, 'Your Majesty, thank you for keeping my seat warm for me.'

16 And yes, I know Napoleon was not really that short – but just go with the joke.

Now King Louis frowns at him, trying to recognise which one of his nobles this might be dressed up. Then the servant who introduced him says again, much slower and clearer, 'Announcing the Emperor of France, Napoleon Bonaparte.'

And you can imagine the silly grin on the King's face slowly sliding into a look of horror. Napoleon! The real Napoleon! Here in New New France! He must have invaded in order to overthrow him and chop his head off!

'I believe that is my seat you are sitting in,' Napoleon says.

But the King does not move.

'My seat,' says Napoleon again.

The King wraps his hands tightly around the armrests, making it clear he is not going to budge.

So picture the two men staring at each other, like the first one to blink will lose, while another of the King's servants scuttles up and whispers into his ear the news he has just heard from the newly arrived ships – that Napoleon has actually been defeated and is in exile.

The King smiles now and is getting ready to call one of his guards to have Napoleon thrown into prison when the servant whispering in his ear also tells him he has brought one thousand members of his personal guards with him – the famous Imperial Guard. The soldiers that have never been defeated in battle. The soldiers who are so tough that they can march all day and night without a meal or a rest, and still win any fight. The soldiers that are so devoted to their leader that they probably swam all the way to New New France.

'Oh,' says the King. Then he asks the servant, 'What do you think I should do?'

'I'll fetch a second chair,' the man says.

And that is how Napoleon and King Louis the 16th end up sitting in separate chairs at either end of the small palace room, glaring at each other every day, and arguing about what they should have painted on the panels outside the windows.

CHAPTER 28

Why having two rulers is never a very good idea

I can tell you that history shows that having two rulers is never a very good idea. Especially when they don't much like each other. Every day is an argument over breakfast, lunch and dinner. They argue over whether an Emperor outranks a King, or whether how long you have ruled for is more important. They argue over whether they hate the English or the Russians more. They argue over which of them is taller.

And they play cards a lot and both try and cheat better than the other.

Of course all over the settlement people are dividing into those who support Napoleon and those who support the King, and so even going shopping becomes a contest between them. People are either buying licorice in support of Napoleon or French cakes in support of the King.

The settlement even acquires two competing names Louisville and Napoleonville.

And the colony ends up with two sets of rules for everything. The supporters of Napoleon insist on driving on the right-hand side of the road, and the supporters of the King insist on driving on the left-hand side. There are two different laws that apply to the people – and for those who were just a little bit clever, they would wear a Napoleon tricolour cockade, or that of King Louis the 16th, depending on which law they wanted applied to them.

The cockade was a circular piece of cloth or paper, shaped a bit like a target symbol, using the French tricolours of red, white and blue. It could be worn on your hat or jacket and was made popular during the French revolution. The traditional colours were blue in the centre, surrounded by white and the outside circle was red.

However in New New France, while the Emperor's supporters wear this cockade, the King's supporters turn it around, with a blue outer circle, then white and a red inner circle. And of course soon most settlers are carrying one of each.

So imagine this – the magistrate is sitting there in the local court room and a settler has been brought before him for selling a neighbour 20 sheep but only giving him 19.

'How do you plead?' the magistrate asks.

'Um – pardon, your honour, but before we go on, can you just clarify for me the different charges under Napoleonic or the King's law?'

The magistrate sighs, like this happens all too often. 'Well,' he says, 'under Napoleonic law if you cheated your neighbour you will need to provide the extra sheep and pay a fine as well.'

'I see,' says the settler. 'And under the King's law?'

'Was your neighbour a nobleman?'

'No.'

'And do you have any noble blood?'

'Uh – an uncle on my mother's side was a count. Does that count for something?'

'If you have noble blood you can do what you want. You cannot be held accountable for how you treat a peasant, only if he is a nobleman.'

'In that case I'm going to go with the King's law.' And he places a royalist cockade on his hat. 'I'm a loyal follower of the King.'

'Yes,' says the magistrate, 'I somehow thought you might be.'

I mentioned before how having two rulers is a really bad idea, and the now divided colony of New New France slowly starts going downhill. But here's a thing – history shows that when internal affairs get really, really bad, it is generally time to find (or invent) an enemy and go to war against, and unite your people.

The British did this in the 1980s in the Falklands, the USA has done it too many times to count, and Napoleon is about to do it to the British settlement in New South Scotland.

CHAPTER 28

Having two rulers is a really bad idea?

He is already sick of King Louis teasing him about being a big time general, but not doing anything about the English military presence to their north. Napoleon decides it is time to act. After all, he strongly believes it is his destiny to achieve military greatness (and to get back at anyone who had ever teased him at school). So he makes a vow to throw the English out and claim New South Scotland as Terre Napoleon — or Napolcon Land.

Things in our What If history have suddenly started getting a lot more serious!

CHAPTER 29

It's time to ask what about the women?

Okay, it's time to ask me, what about the women? Where were all the women during this?

Go, on. Ask me.

Okay, to answer your question I have to point out a few issues with standard history that we could perhaps correct in a What If history. The first is that most recorders of history were men and they wrote about very men things, like exploring and being bitten by snakes and fighting each other and getting killed and other terrible but heroic things. From a women's point of view these might be considered very stupid things, of course, and the important things were having children and raising families and trying to convince their fathers and husbands and sons not to go exploring or to go off to war where terrible things were going to happen to them.

There is a famous quote that is sometimes attributed to Winston Churchill, the British Prime Minister during

World War Two. He was supposed to have said that History is written by the victors. This means that those who win the war or do the exploring tell their own side of things and ignore any other side. Like who in the 18th and 19th century told the stories of First Nations Australians? Not many people.

Or who was writing about women?

Again, not many people.

So let's fix that.

When Napoleon went into exile in New New France, he not only brought his wife Marie Louise of Austria with him, but his former wife Josephine. Now you might think that was trouble enough, but things got really tricky when they met Marie Antoinette – the King's wife.

In fact they were all three of them named Marie, as Josephine's real name was Marie Josèphe Rose Tascher de La Pagerie. Added to that both Marie Antoinette and Marie Louise were Austrians, and were distantly related, which gave them something in common over Marie Josèphe. But Marie Louise and Marie Josèphe had their marriages to Napoleon in common. But of course Marie Josèphe and Marie Antoinette had little in common, and Marie Josèphe had a grudge with Marie Antoinette as her first husband, Alexandre, had once refused to introduce her to the Queen at court. However Marie Antoinette and Marie Josèphe were much closer to each other in ages, at 62 and 54, while Marie Louise was only 26.

Are you keeping up with all this?

Anyway, the three Maries all found unity in their grudges against Napoleon. Marie Josèphe because he divorced her, Marie Louise because she had never much liked him (and in fact her father joined forces to defeat him after his retreat from Moscow). And Marie Antoinette because he represented the revolutionary forces that overthrew her and her husband.

So here we have the three most powerful women in France – none of them born in France itself, all now living in New New France together, with plenty of discontent at their lot in life.

An important question is, do we use our What If history to have them preoccupied with teaming up against the other, much as their husbands spent their lives doing politically? Or do we have them actually put their heads together and start making the decisions about ruling New New France that needed to be made – while the King and Emperor were busy trying to see who has the highest chair in the room?

If we take the first path, we could mirror the battles and alliances of Europe between the women and the changing way they form alliances. For instance, first Marie Josèphe and Marie Louise gang up on Marie Antoinette over something, and then Marie Antoinette and Marie Louise gang up on Marie Josèphe over something else.

Who lends who their best gown? Who hides the nicest food from the others? Who works hard to undermine the other's husband by spreading rumours about him? Or who finally, gets tired of all the silly little bickering and games and proposes the three women do something about the poor standard of education in the colony and the lack of a decent hospital?

The three of them are not short of money – care of the King and Emperor admittedly – but they still had access to it. So What If they decided to put their energies into building schools and hospitals and so on? What If they even got just a little bit competitive about it, and which ever project they chose, education, health and welfare, they strived to make theirs just a little bit better than that of the other two?

Can you picture what mealtimes must have been like?

There is this long, long table that takes up the length of one of the rooms in the brick house they call a palace. The Emperor Napoleon sits at one end, on a chair that is lifted up a little on bricks, and King Louis the 16th sits at the other end, on a chair lifted up on blocks of wood. Marie Antoinette sits beside the King, Marie Louise sits next to Napoleon and Marie Josèphe sits somewhere in the middle. The men refuse to talk to each other, of course, nor even acknowledge the presence of the other.

Settlers have been trying to lobby the two men all day to bring to their attention the fact that there is a drought and the farms are not growing enough food. But they are too obsessed with getting a higher, better chair than the other, and cannot focus on the matter.

The settlers then bring the matter to the attention of the three Maries, and they decide they must act. Cleverly.

'This meat is a little dry, don't you think?' says Marie Louis to the Emperor.

'Yes, it is dry,' he says. 'We should do something about it.'

'I was trying to add up how long your reign had been?' Marie Antoinette asks the King. 'Can you recall?'

'Huh,' he says. 'I cannot remember the last time I truly reigned.'

'The land here needs your reign,' she tells him. 'It cannot survive without it.'

'It needs your reign more,' Marie Louise whispers to Napoleon.

He nods his head. 'True.'

'I find the land here so very harsh,' says Marie Josèphe. 'I cannot imagine how the farmers manage to grow crops when it fails to rain.'

Neither the King nor the Emperor look at her.

'I have an idea,' Marie Antoinette says softly. 'What if we purchase goods from the Dutch traders to give to the farmers who are suffering the effects of drought? Tell them it is a gift from their King who reigns over them.'

'How much will that cost?' King Louis asks.

'I could find a trader who would throw in a throne as a part of the deal. One a little higher than this one.'

'That would be splendid,' he whispers back. 'But make sure that gutter-snipe Napoleon fellow doesn't find out about it.'

And Marie Louis whispers to Napoleon, 'I think you should try and win over some of the King's supporters.'

'How do you propose I do that?' he asks.

'Many of the original colonists are having trouble growing crops. It is so dry that there is barely enough wheat to make French loaves.'

'And what should I do about it?' he asks. 'Reform the weather?'

'Buy grain from the Spanish traders,' she says. 'Give it to them as a gift and tell the farmers it comes from the Emperor.'

'And do you think they would come across to our side?'

'I'm sure of it.'

'Well, perhaps.'

'And your followers will build you an even taller and grander chair than this one as thanks.'

He nods his head. 'I like this idea. But make sure that pimple-bottomed King doesn't find out about it.'

CHAPTER 30

Preparing for the invasion of New New London

So back to the war between the English and the French – which may have now ended in Europe but was alive and well in the great south lands of New New France and New South Scotland.

The first thing Napoleon starts doing in preparation for his invasion of New New London, is to send spies there to report back to him on its defences and military strengths and so on. But the British aren't so stupid as to answer every question a shady looking merchant with a French accent asks about their troops. So they tell them numbers that are two or three times higher than the actual numbers (as well as lying about the weather, the growing traffic problems and the amount of deadly, huge, hairy spiders and snakes that live there).

CHAPTER 30

The idea was to make Napoleon think they had more soldiers stationed there than they actually did. But while it might have seemed clever at first, it was actually a dumb idea, because it meant that Napoleon's invasion plans involved more troops than he might otherwise have sent.

So let's say the number of soldiers at New New London was about 500 and let's say that Napoleon had brought

1,000 of his elite Imperial Guard with him. If he had known there were only 500 English soldiers at New New London, he would have left some of the Guard behind to keep a close eye on the King and protect New New France from the Spanish, or Austrians or the Russians or whoever. But as he thought there were about 1,500 British troops, he took all his guards with him and he made careful plans to surprise the British so they could not use their advantage of numbers.

These days it is pretty clear that if you want to sneak into Sydney you just take a bus or a train from anywhere, and while everyone who comes by sea or by airplane is searched and x-rayed and scrutinised by security forces, those on the buses and trains just hop off and wander freely around the city.

Unfortunately there were no buses or trains in Napoleon's time so he has to either march overland to reach the settlement, or sail around by sea. Knowing that an overland march hadn't gone too well when trying to invade Russia, he thinks that a bit risky. But he also knows his track record for sea-based successes isn't that great either. Despite having a strong navy Napoleon had his butt kicked by the British at the Battle of the Nile, and also at the Battle of Trafalgar, and he had to keep postponing his great sea-borne invasion of Britain, despite several close attempts at it.

Battle of the Nile Battle of Trafalgar

So Napoleon decides on a combined land and sea approach. He is going to sail his army around close to New New London, land them to the south of the colony, and then sail up to the main harbour and make threatening gestures and fire cannons at the British.

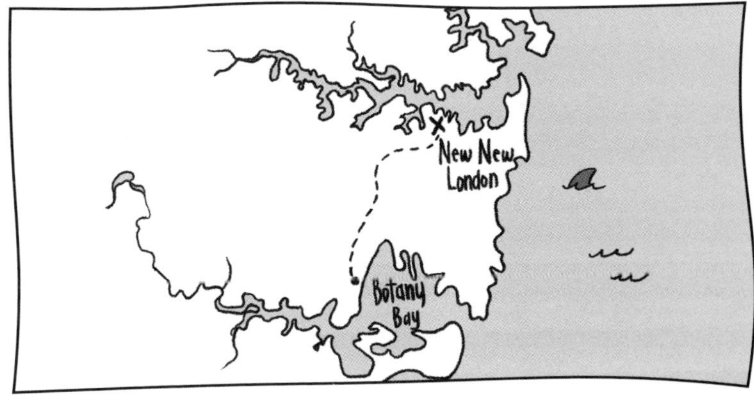

They will respond by sending all their soldiers to defend the harbour mouth, leaving the settlement unguarded for his rear-attack. It is a good plan. No, it is a great plan. *C'est Magnifique!*[17]

Until the King hears about it. He thinks it too tricky and lacks the honest approach to battle that a true nobleman would engage in. Napoleon tells him that he would be happy to listen to the King's advice on battle if he had any experience of it to give advice on.

The King replies that he'd be happy to listen to Napoleon's advice on ruling a nation if he had any experience to base it on. Napoleon then throws his deck of marked cards at the King and the two men have to be separated by their servants, who all encourage Napoleon to go and invade the British colony as soon as he can, to make their lives a bit easier.

17 Translation: That's like awesome, dude!

CHAPTER 31

The Invasion Fleet arrives at Botany Bay

So this is what happens.

First the ships are gotten ready. That meant cleaning out all the ships and drunken sailors[18], and getting the cannons cleared of cobwebs, and the holds loaded up with provisions for an army. Most of these have to be bought from the local farmers who all agree, as farmers have throughout history, that sending out an invasion force is good for business (though it should be mentioned that having an invasion force invade you is universally bad for business).

18 *Singing* Throw them in the harbour and they'll smell less-o.

Then the soldiers have to be gotten into good shape. They have to be cleaned up and drilled in marching, and their officers have to be taken through the secret plans. That is a tricky thing about secret plans, the more people you need to tell them to, to ensure they work properly, the less secret they become. And as much as Napoleon has sent spies to New New London, the British have their spies in New New France.

But again, the French aren't so stupid as to answer every question put to them by merchants with strong English accents who ask why the ships are being made ready, and why the troops are being drilled? They tell them that they are going to claim New Zealand for France, and need a strong army to defeat the Maori warriors there. They also lie about their gloomy weather in winter, the quality of coffee in their cafes, and what it is really like having two rulers.

There may have been a few British spies dumb enough to fall for this, but most of them report back that the French are preparing to invade New New London. So Governor Davey starts getting ready. True to form, rather than make any decision, he puts on his brown trousers and orders his junior officers to make all the preparations, while he locks himself in his office and works on designing a heavily fortified bird bath.

And of course some of his officers immediately apply for sick leave, while the others make plans for moving all their troops to the two pincer shaped headlands that make up the opening to Sydney Harbour. Oops – I mean the New New London Harbour!

Which Napoleon's spies duly report back on.

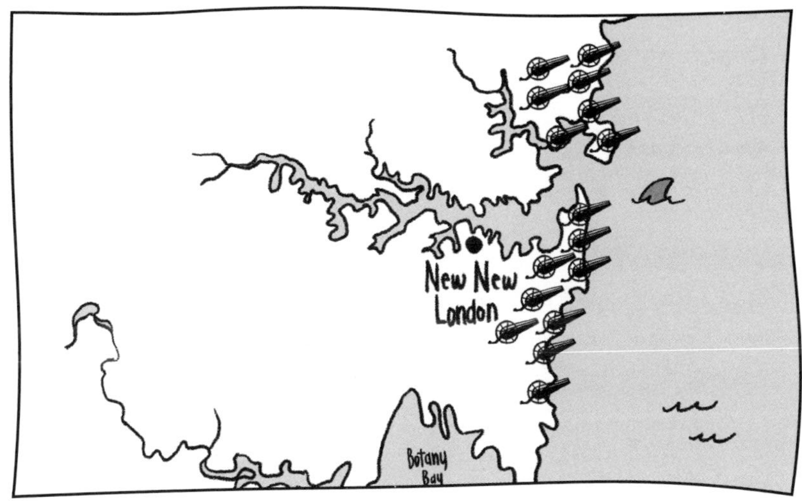

Napoleon is pretty happy about all this, of course, and is thinking that if he is able to overthrow the British all the royalists who support the King might come over to his side. Then he could overthrow Louis the 16th as well, becoming Emperor of the whole country here.

He likes the thought of that, for when he looks on the map the distance between the west and east coasts of the Australian mainland is about the same distance between Paris and Moscow. And that means he will have conquered an area the same size, making up for his Russian defeat!

'Oiu!' he says to himself, punching his fist up high – also inventing the air punch.

Well they finally get the invasion fleet ready, which pleases King Louis the 16th enormously, for he hopes that the English will win the battle and he'll be rid of Napoleon for good. Maybe they'll exile him somewhere even more remote – like the unknown land of ice to the south. He's been hearing stories of it, and somebody had to go and explore it. Why not Napoleon?

The day the invasion fleet sails out of New New France is a grand one (play sound effects of trumpets and drums and men singing). But the Bass Strait – sorry the La Perouse Strait – is renowned for fickle weather. The invasion fleet has barely gotten past Van Diemen's Land and indicates to make a left turn, when a huge wind comes gusting up from the south, blowing the ships every which way.

Normally this wouldn't be such a problem as you would just shorten your sails, or tuck them in shorter, and ride the storm out, pushing you faster and further on your way north. But different sized ships respond differently to such storms and particularly at night it is hard to know where everyone is. The important thing about an invasion fleet is that it works best when all the ships arrive at the place of invasion at the same time, and it just isn't as effective if they all get there on different days like they might in the Sydney to Hobart Yacht Race.

So Napoleon has to gather all his ships together and make sure he hasn't lost any of them, and then he has to wait for the soldiers of the Imperial Guard to recover from their seasickness. Then they finally get on with the invasion once more (repeat sound effects of trumpets and drums and men singing).

The rest of the trip north to New New London is fairly uneventful, if you don't count Napoleon getting a bit of sunburn – which most historians for some reason never seem to comment on, because it can really addle your brain. Historians like to talk about when Napoleon had a bad cold, or the flu, or diarrhoea, and how it affected his decisions – but getting too much sun is seriously overlooked.

Well the invasion fleet makes good time, and they catch a few nice fish, see some whales blowing waterspouts and play games like counting the seagulls.

‘Eighteen.’

‘No you counted that one already.’

‘No I counted that one – the white one over there.’

‘The one with the orange legs?’

‘Yes. That one.’

‘I’m sure you counted that one already.’

‘Which one?’

And then, finally, eventually, at last, they are close to New New Sydney and prepared to invade. Napoleon looks through his telescope and can’t see any sign of defences. That is good, but a bit odd, he thinks. He has been told by his spies that the English had mounted a cannon near the entrance to the harbour (but also that they didn’t have any dangerous snakes and spiders at all there). However he can see no sign of them. Nor can he see any troops. Or houses. Or anything.

He calls his fleet admiral to him and asks him, 'Are you sure we have found the right place?'

'*Oui, mon empereur,*[19]' the man tells him. 'I have been here before.'

'But where is New New Sydney?'

'Um – it is just north of us. The plan was to let our men ashore here in Botany Bay, as you planned it.'

'Of course,' says Napoleon, suddenly recalling the plan. Clearly he had gotten too much sun and it was making his normal military genius a little addled. 'I'm just testing you,' he says.

(Which is a very timely reminder, dear readers, that this is what happens when you try to lead an invasion fleet somewhere without your hat on. A good lesson in life is never invade without your hat!)

'Oui, mon Emperor,' says the man and salutes.

'Bring us into the bay,' Napoleon orders, even though the ships are already making their way into the bay.

'One more thing,' he calls to the fleet admiral. 'Why did the British call it Botany Bay?'

19 Translation: Yes boss.

'I believe it has something to do with the prickly plants that grow here being very rough on your botty, if you try to wipe yourself with them,' he said.

'Of course,' says Napoleon.

Then the ships are all in the bay, and they make their way over to the southern shore (pretty much where Captain Cook had landed), and something very interesting happens. You might remember that when the Cookster had landed here in 1770, two of the locals came out with spears and opposed him from landing. Well a similar thing happens again! Two of the locals see the French invasion fleet's boats coming ashore and go down to the beach to oppose them.

They wait until the boats have landed and then step up and tell them, in a mix of broken English and sign language, that this is private property and a no landing zone, and they will need to pay a fine and also move along and find an approved landing zone somewhere further around the bay.

CHAPTER 31

The locals have clearly learned a few important things from the British settlers in the intervening years since Cook had been there.

Once the French have found a suitable landing zone (further around the bay), the French soldiers are all brought ashore and they line up into columns for inspection. They look formidable, as the Imperial Guard always does. Then they set off on their march across land to the settlement, and the ships go back out to sea to begin part two of their invasion plan.

And if you want to know what being a soldier was like in those days, it isn't as much fun as it looks on TV. All that background music and drums as you fire at the enemy with your musket and never miss, but the enemy always miss when they shoot at you, right? Well it is not much like that at all. You are tired and dirty and smelly from all the marching and probably haven't slept well from having to camp out at nights. And when the enemy line up against you it looks like you are outnumbered ten to one, regardless of their actual numbers. And you are so afraid that you tremble all over and just want to step off behind a bush and go to the toilet, but you aren't allowed to. You have to stay there and wait while the enemy fire cannon balls at you. And if they hit the person next to you you're splattered with pieces of him, leaving guts and gore all over you. And then the enemy come marching at you and the trembling gets even worse, for it feels like when you shoot at them the shots always miss, but when they shoot at you every shot hits someone. And the bang of the guns is noisy and smells of gunpowder which gets stuck in your nose and throat like a bitter fog. And the closer the enemy get the more you are convinced that the next shot is going to hit you, and the more afraid you get, and the harder it is to even hold your gun straight.

And how do I know this exactly? Well I know this because in researching this book I spent a week as a member of Napoleon's army, fighting the English.

And do you know what else? Yes, that's actually another What If dodgy fact[20]. I did spend an evening watching a documentary about the Napoleonic wars on YouTube though.

20 You're probably spotting these much quicker now, yes?

CHAPTER 32

But where are the troops?

So Napoleon and his invasion fleet sail right up to the entrance to New New London harbour and start firing their cannons at the fortifications there. Napoleon is admiring the location of the settlement, seeing it is very well protected by a narrow inlet into a wide open harbour, ringed by large cliffs that are much better for building forts on than the sand banks down in New New Paris.

And it would be much warmer here in the winter, he thinks. And protected from those wretched southerly squalls. And there are no horrible snakes and spiders, according to his spies. The more he thinks about it, the more he is determined to conquer this settlement and make it his new home. King Louis can stay down in New New France, and he will name this place New New New France!

But his thoughts are interrupted by cannons firing shots down on him.

And here is something you should know about cannons, if they are up on high cliffs they can more easily shoot down on a ship below than a ship can shoot up at them. Most ship's cannons are designed to shoot at something the same height, like another ship. But to shoot up at a high target requires building new cannon mounts that let you raise the cannon very high.

And if I told you that Napoleon had started his military career in the artillery, you would probably guess that Napoleon knew every single thing there was to know about cannons, and was ready for this. If only his spies had remembered to tell him how high the cliffs were.

Shot after shot rains down on them until two ships are sunk and Napoleon has to be convinced to pull the other ships further back out to sea.

It is frustrating, of course, as he was busting to engage the enemy and he did fire a few cannon shots into the cliff faces, but he knows it doesn't matter. He only has to wait until his soldiers have marched into the settlement from the south and captured it. He is only there to create a diversion, after all. Then his troops will send up a rocket to inform him of their victory. And after that he will sail his ships victoriously in between the cliffs and New New London will be his.

He is wondering if he might call the new city he builds there Napoleonopolis or Bonapartville, when one of his officers comes and tells him the rocket signal is long overdue.

The Emperor looks at the setting sun. The man is right. The day is getting on and all he can see are the cannon blasts from the British guns on the cliffs, as they keep firing at him, hoping to get a lucky hit.

And then another one of those cursed southerly winds appears. What was it with the weather conspiring against him, he wonders? It again throws his ships into disarray, sending them all over the place in the gathering darkness. That is a problem, for normally they would light signal lamps for the other ships to find each other – but if they light them tonight it will just help the British to know where to fire their cannons at.

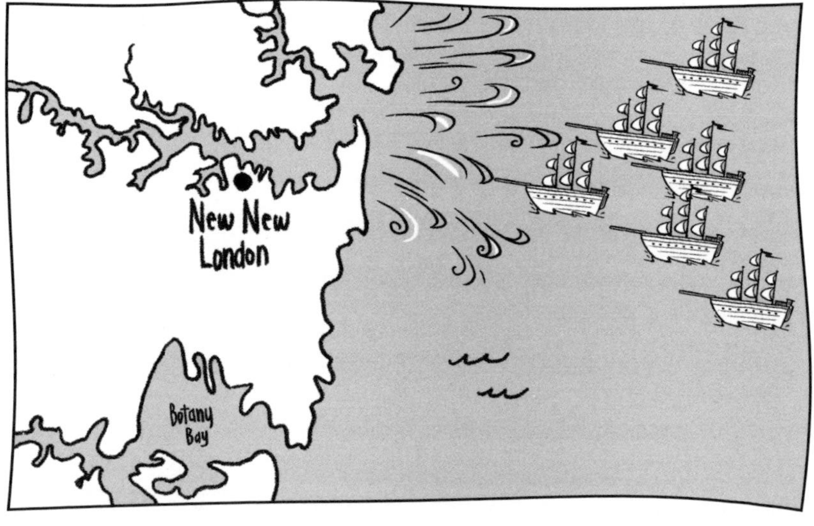

But without lights there is risk that some of his ships might bump into each other in the darkness.

And you just know that is going to happen, right?

Two ships do hit each other and are so badly damaged they aren't fit to take part in the battle anymore.

So Napoleon's ships bob around on the ocean all night long waiting for the winds to drop, waiting for the British to stop firing at them, waiting for the Imperial Guard to send up a victory rocket, waiting to not bump into each other. Waiting, waiting, waiting.

By first light Napoleon can see his scattered fleet coming back together. He can see the damage to the two ships that had collided. He can see that everyone is confused as to why a rocket had not been fired by his troops ashore.

And no one knows what to do.

Except for Napoleon of course. He wants to charge into the harbour, flying the French flag proudly and chasing the British away with just his bravery and determination. But he knows the cannons either side of the harbour entrance will blow them all to pieces before he gets far into the harbour.

He curses and eventually orders the ships back to Botany Bay, to find out what had happened to his troops.

It takes a few hours to get there, and when they come into the bay, there is no sign of his troops. Napoleon is perplexed. If his men had run into heavy defences they would have sent a messenger back here for him.

And that means all he can do is wait. Wait. Wait. Wait.

He paces the decks of his ships cursing and chewing the nail off his thumb until about 4 o'clock in the afternoon, when he sees the first distinctive blue coats of his guardsmen emerging onto the beach. Exactly where they had set out from, down beyond the no landing zone.

He looks through his telescope and sees that the men look like they had been in a major battle. They are stumbling and their clothes are in tatters. Many are without backpacks. Or hats!

(And we know what happens if you don't wear your hat during an invasion, yes?)

Had the British ambushed them? Had the locals attacked them? How was it possible that his Imperial Guard had been turned back? It was unthinkable!

CHAPTER 32

'Someone take me ashore!' he commands. 'I must know what happened.'

So Napoleon is rowed ashore and is able to stand there on the sands of New New Scotland at last, as if he was a victorious conqueror. But the feeling doesn't last long. A small group of officers of the Imperial Guard come over to him and salute.

'Report!' he demands.

And one of the officers says, 'Um – I think we should stand over here a bit. Near the rest of the men We'll get a fine if we stand here. It is a no landing zone.'

And Napoleon screams, 'We will stand where I am standing! I said report!'

Then all the officers start talking all at once, in mumbles, none wishing to be the one who tells the full story and receives their Emperor's wrath.

'We could not navigate.'

'There were no paths or roads to follow.'

'The bushland is devilish and impossible to march through.'

'We could not determine our way'

'The trees have prickles that seized our hats.'

'We were so hot we drank all our water.'

'It became dark and we still didn't know where we were going.'

'We could hear the noise of cannon but couldn't tell which direction it was coming from.'

'We tried our best.'

'We were lost.'

'We marched all through the night.'

'It was stifling hot.'

'And there were snakes.'

'And spiders.'

'Huge hairy spiders!'

'And snakes. Lots of snakes.'

'And giant ants that would crawl into your trousers if you sat down.'

'And weird beasts that called out to us from the darkness.'

'And mosquitoes. So many mosquitoes.'

'When the sun came up we still didn't know where we were.'

'And black and white birds swooped us.'

'The few natives we saw ran from us.'

'If we had caught one we might have had a guide.'

'How can the British live in a land like this?'

'Then we realised we were on the path we had made the first day.'

'It was like the retreat from Moscow.'

'Except for the terrible heat rather than the terrible cold.'

'Yes, just like Moscow.'

'Did we mention there were snakes?'

'Can we come back and try this another time?' the highest-ranking officer asks. 'I lost my hat and the sun has made me feel very faint.'

'And I wiped my bottom on a plant that proved very prickly,' says another officer. 'It makes it very hard to march.'

Napoleon wants to shout at them some more and order them to turn around and go back to New New London. Wants to tell his ships to go back and bombard the defences, no matter how out of reach they are. Wants to keep trying until they get it right. But, the fact is, the sun has now given him a really, really terrible headache. Curse this infernal land. He finds he just wants to go back to his chair in New New Paris, and sit out of the sun, and insult King Louis. And then a lie down and eat a bag of licorice.

'An invasion of this land would cost us too much,' he says. 'I think we shall declare it a tie.'

Now I know those readers looking forward to a big battle scene might be feeling a little disappointed right about now – but don't despair, there is still a bit of the book to go. And that means there might still be time to fit a big battle in.

No promises – just saying.

And anyway, no matter how disappointed you are, Napoleon was a lot more disappointed, I can tell you!

CHAPTER 33

The English put up their Dukes

So what happens in our What If history next?

Plenty!

Firstly, Napoleon goes back to New New Paris with stories of his great victory in New New London. (He really did this after his defeat in Egypt in real life. He went home and told everyone it was a great victory and he was hailed as a hero).

And the British, pondering the French attack, decide they need a better military mind down there minding the place than Governor Davey. And who do they choose? A man named Arthur Wellesley. You might not have heard of him by that name, but he was also known as the Duke of Wellington! And I suspect you might have heard of him.

He was the man who in real life not only booted Napoleon's butt at Waterloo with his Wellington boots, but had spent many years before that fighting him across

Europe. If anyone was able to stop Napoleon in real history or in our What If history, it would be Artie!

If you look up his picture you'll see he looks a lot like that kid who is good at everything at school – and knows it.

The Duke of Wellington

Also, politicians in England are worried that he was positioning himself to become Prime Minister of the country, and want him out of the way. Far, far out of the way!

So he arrives at the colony of New New London in 1820, about ten years after the settlement was established, and his first task is to fire Governor Davey. He takes great delight in that.

'You're fired!' he tells him.

'I'm what?' Governor Davey asks.

'Fired. You're sacked. Dismissed. Terminated. Discharged. You are being given the chop. The axe. The shove. The bounce. Pack your bags and go.'

'Oh,' says Governor Davey. 'Can I interest you in bird baths? They are quite lovely and I can you have one quite cheap?'

'Let go. Laid off. Not needed. Redundant,' continues the Duke of Wellington.

Governor Davey – or former-Governor Davey – gets the hint and goes to pack his bags for the voyage back to England.

The Duke – or Governor Wellington – starts off his rule by increasing the defences of the settlement and sending out exploratory parties to better map the lands around them. He is convinced that Napoleon will invade again, and will do a better job of it this time, and he wants to be ready.

One of the men he sends out exploring is named Matthew Flinders. He is an up-and-coming mapmaker and navigator, who proves more than up to the task. Indeed rather than just mapping the bits of the territory of New New Scotland, he ends up sailing right around the continent and mapping it all.

Matthew Flinders

And if you look up a picture of him you'll see he looks a lot like the kid who was the second smartest in the class, but really, really wanted to be the smartest, and became a huge try-hard as a result. Anyway, after sailing right around the continent he names it Australia. But Governor Wellington says it will never catch on.

And down in New New France when Napoleon is told of the name, he says, 'Why would they call it Austria? That is stupid. There is already an Austria. I know because I conquered it. Maybe they should call it New Austria. Or if there is already a New Austria, then New New Austria. Maybe this is a challenge to me? Asking me if I dare invade them again. Or are the English just being stupid? Maybe I should send my wife to them as an envoy of Austria and totally confuse them.'

Meanwhile the Governor Duke Dude was finding that the quality of soldiers that had been sent to New New London were clearly not the best of the best. Most of the men just wanted to sit on the beaches all day playing cricket and drinking rum. For under the leadership of Governor Davey, the military had become rather rebellious and full of their own importance. Particularly since they felt they had defeated Napoleon!

They refused to oversee convicts and they refused to take part in work details and they demanded first purchasing rights off any ship that sailed into the colony.

That meant they could buy the cargo first and then sell it to the settlers at enormous profits.

In real life things weren't that much different, actually. The New South Wales Corp had become known as the Rum Corps, because they took over the trading of rum – which became the informal currency of the colony. As we know, Governor Arthur Phillip wasn't such a bad sort, but when he went back to England in ill health in 1792 his second in command, Major Grose, took over. And that was a gross mistake. If you find a picture of him you'll see he looks a lot like the kid in school who regularly stole cakes from everyone else's lunch boxes.

Major Grose

He abolished all the civilian courts and appointed military courts and gave all the administrative powers to the military. He then gave his military buddies large land grants and pretty much continued the abuse of power that happens every time the military step in to take over governing a country.

You can look through all the history books you want to on this, but there are very, very, very few examples of things working out for the better when the military take over government.

And if you think about it, why would they be any good at governing? They have been trained for a different type of job. It would be like giving a shonky businessman the Presidency of a country and expecting he wouldn't run it like a shonky business! The military ran everything like it was a military campaign that they had to win at all costs.

So, things went from bad to worse as a series of governors was appointed and tried to stop the rum trade, culminating in Governor Bligh – the same man who was captain of the Bounty where the crew mutinied.

Well the same thing happened again in New South Wales. The Rum Corps were not happy at the way he was trying to curb their power and they mutinied too. They would have put him in a small boat with not quite enough water and food and let him sail 6,700 kilometres to safety – but since they weren't at sea, and he had already overcome that after the Bounty mutiny, the soldiers instead marched to Government House and arrested him.

Well they put him under house arrest, which is a lot better than being put into a jail cell. Then they proceeded to give themselves and all their mates the best jobs and to pardon each other for any wrongdoing and so on.

The British Government were not too impressed with this turn of events though, and after a lot of silly business in the colony they decided to replace the entire New South Wales corps with an entirely new military corps, and a new Governor who could oversee some return to sensible rule. That was Major-General Lachlan Macquarie.

But back to our What If Wellington.

He was not the type of man you'd attempt to put under house arrest like Bligh, and it was said that he was so tough that he slept on the floor on bare floorboards, ate rocks for breakfast and his steely stare could wound a man at 50 paces. You probably won't find that on Wikipedia, but just trust me on this. In researching this book I tried living just like that and accidentally wounded the postman and garbageman just by staring at them.

Well, okay, I made all that up after the floorboards bit. But he was a tough character!

Pretty soon Wellington has the troops drilling and digging trenches and carrying heavy muskets with heavy packs up and down hills in the heat. Because every good general knows that the best way to beat an enemy is to impress them with your ability to carry a heavy musket and heavy pack up and down a hill on a hot day, right!

The troops aren't very happy about this turn of affairs, but they are pretty afraid of the Duke's deadly stare, so go back to obeying orders.

Napoleon has spies in the colony of course, usually French men pretending to be Spanish traders. They would show up on their ship to sell Spanish dollar shop things to the English – like, well Flamenco shoes and Spanish beer or anything else that the Spanish made that English people might actually want to buy. They report to Napoleon that his old enemy from the Spanish wars is in charge of New New London, and turning it into a bit of a fortress.

Napoleon curses his luck and has his men raise his chair a few centimetres higher than King Louis' chair.

He knows there is little chance of successfully invading New New London with the Duke in charge there – so he turns his creative energies to trying to perfect the invention of the first flushing toilet in the colonies. But even that was proving difficult as he was being defeated by a water loo.

(Sorry – probably the worst joke yet.)[21]

21 Maybe. No promises.

CHAPTER 34

The fall of Kings and Emperors

So let's get to the last bits of this story and what happens to everyone – before we get to that big battle I promised you. First let's turn to Napoleon and his two Maries, and King Louis and his one Marie.

In real life Napoleon escaped from his exile on the island of Elba in the Mediterranean Sea after less than a year. He came back to France in March 1815, and as he marched towards Paris, more and more people came out to greet and join him. He reached the capital with an army of about 6,000 men, and took over running the place again.

And he was more determined than ever to teach a lesson to the Allied armies for teasing him. He set about invading the countries around France all over again. Until the British and Prussians stopped him at the battle of Waterloo though it was actually a closer call than you might think.

And Napoleon was again sent into exile.

This time he was sent to a very small island in the remote southern Atlantic Ocean named Saint Helena. This place was so remote that the British had used it as a place to dump zombies.

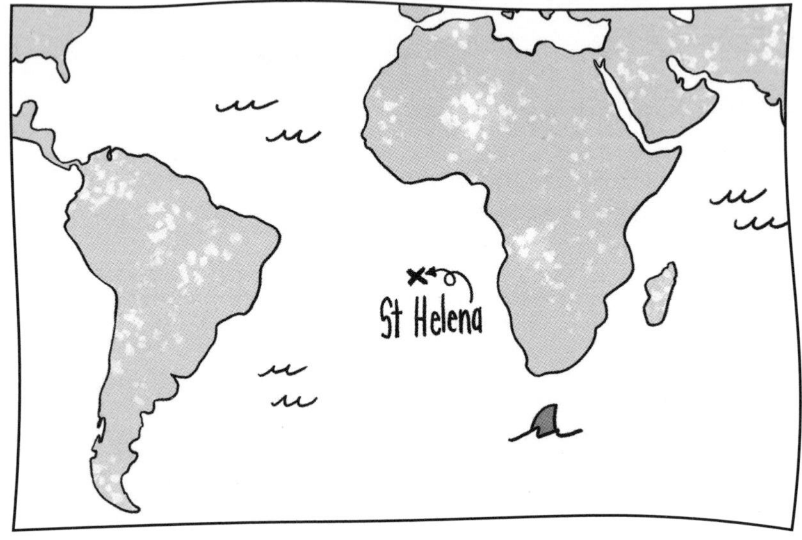

Sorry – I just made that up.

But it is so small and remote that if you go looking for it on Google Maps even you're going to have trouble finding it. It is a tiny speck of an island in the middle of a big, big ocean that is largely without islands. It is a perfect island prison for a crazy French Emperor who has a desire to conquer the world.

Napoleon lived out his last six years there, despite several crazy schemes to rescue him, including one using a primitive submarine. But they all came to nothing. He died, perhaps of stomach cancer, or perhaps from having been poisoned, or perhaps of boredom, in 1821 – when he was aged 51.

But let's see how things ended for the Emperor in our What If story, and go back to that throne room in New New France, with King Louis and Napoleon up on their thrones, scowling at each other.

They are two old men now, who have reached a reflective time of life, and have started thinking about how they might finish their days. Wondering about all the things they never did. All the countries they never invaded. All the pastries they never ate.

It is a constant source of disappointment to both of them that the motherland of France has constantly failed to call either of them home to lead the nation. France had become, of all things, a democratic republic, like the USA! The French decided they didn't really need a King nor an Emperor, and preferred to have a President to rule the country.

The other countries of Europe are worried about this, of course. As much as they had been worried about the French Revolution, and as much as they had been worried about Napoleon's rule, and as much as they had been worried about pretty much everything the French ever did. So they watched and hoped it would never catch on their own countries.

By the year 1825 King Louis the 16th is 71 and getting very feeble. He can barely remember what day it is and who is who and some days he would even climb up into Napoleon's throne. Which drives Napoleon into crazy rants and curses until the King's aides take him back over to his own side of the throne room.

Also their respective thrones have slowly gotten higher and higher, until they needed taller and taller ladders to climb up into them. They are so high now that if the King wore his crown he had to bend his head a little so it wouldn't scratch the ceiling.

Both men still spend most of their days glaring at each other. But on this fateful day of the death of Kings (or a King and an Emperor), King Louis has a moment of forgetfulness and turns his head to look out the windows and sees the lawns and fountains of Versailles there. Yes, they had finally found somebody who could paint a decent painting, and coupled with Louis's failing vision, and fading memory, he believes he is looking at the actual fountains and gardens of Versailles.

For a moment he is no longer an aged and exiled King whose knees hurt too much to walk very far, but he is his younger self back at court. He smiles and decides it is a very pleasant day to take a stroll around the gardens and free himself from having to try and pretend to be making decisions of State.

And he rises and takes a step forward to walk out of the throne room. But that step is a very, very, very high one, and to the shock and horror of everyone in the room (well everyone except Napoleon), he falls to the stone floor and with a loud cracking sound, having broken his neck.

The whole room is silent with every courtier and servant looking at the body of the King aghast. If this had been a Shakespeare play there would have been thunder and lightning. But the only sound is that of one man laughing.

Napoleon Bonaparte! Once the scourge of Europe, now sitting at the other end of the throne room in his equally high throne and having just witnessed the funniest thing of his life. The fall of a King! He starts laughing so hard in fact that he cannot breathe properly and reaches out a hand for a glass of water or wine or something. But he is so high up on his throne that nothing is within reach and the further he leans, the more precarious his perch is. Until – you guessed it – he too topples from his throne and hits the stone floor with an equally loud crack. At 56 years old Napoleon Bonaparte is dead.

At last he and Louis are equals.

CHAPTER 35
So many Maries

So now might have been a good opportunity for New New France to try and fix up the mess that the two rulers had made of the place, but unfortunately there were two heirs who both put their hands up to be the next ruler.

This gets a bit complex, so try and follow it as we go. King Louis and Marie Antoinette had four children – Marie Thérèse, Louis Joseph, Louis Charles, and Sophie. Unfortunately Louis Joseph had died at the age of seven and Sophie had died before she was one. That left Marie Thérèse (yes, another Marie) and Louis Charles (yes, another Louis).

Now in real life Louis Charles had died aged ten, after having caught tuberculosis upon his imprisonment by the Revolutionary Government. But in our What If story he has not spent any time in prison. That means he could have lived a longer and fuller life in New New France, and in 1825 he is 40 years old and the royalist heir to the New New French throne.

But Napoleon also has an heir – Napoleon II, who is now 14 years old. But if history has taught us anything, it is don't leave a teenager in charge of things!

So while Louis Charles is getting ready to ascend his father's throne and take over the colony as King, Marie Louise is giving Napoleon II a boost up into his own father's throne. She also has an equally high one being built next to it for her to sit in as advisor to the Emperor. She says that it is her duty and her role to make the decisions of state until he is old enough to rule in his own right.

Of course he says, 'Aw muuuuum! You never let me have any fun.'

And she says, 'Shhh. Don't backtalk your mother or there will be no sweets after dinner.'

And he sulks and pouts (just like his father had sulked and pouted in fact).

Marie Louise is now an eligible widow, and at 34 years old is the youngest of all the four Maries. Marie Antoinette, King Louis the 16th's wife, is 70 – and only interested in baking and nagging her two children about having some grandchildren. Marie Josèphe, Napoleon's first wife, was 62 and also a bit old for matters of state, being more interested in her garden. And Marie Thérèse, Marie Antoinette's daughter, was 47 and more interested in going to book club than most anything else.

Marie Thérèse

But What If King Louis the 17th proposes marriage to Marie Louise (Napoleon's second wife, remember), and What If she agrees?[22] I mean there was a distinct shortage of royals in the colony to consider marrying, and if she says yes, that will enable her to be Queen of New New France, rather than just adviser to her young son the Emperor-in-waiting.

Keeping up so far?

And if Marie Louise was Queen, then her son Napoleon II might well become heir and next in line for the throne. Or she might even have some other children with the new King and one of them might become the next King.

They have a lot in common, after all. They have both spent a lot of their life in New New France and understand its peculiar climate and animals and so on. Napoleon has driven them both crazy, and being French they both hate the English.

And if they married they could abolish all the silly divisive rules in the colony and all drive on the same side of the road and all use the same units of measurement and so on.

Maybe.

22 In case you have lost track, he is 40 and she is 34.

CHAPTER 35

What do you do with a problem like Maria?

Maria (or Marie in French) was just about as popular a name in Austria as Louis was in French. Marie Antoinette's mother, Maria Theresa, the Queen of Austria and all its many dominions had two sisters named Maria Anna and Maria Amalia. She gave birth to 13 children that survived infancy - most of them were women and all named Maria:

Maria Elisabeth

Maria Anna

Maria Carolina

Maria Christina

Maria Elisabeth

Maria Amalia

Maria Johanna

Maria Josepha

Maria Antonia – who become better known as Marie Antoinette.

I'm sure that calling all the children in for dinner must have been really easy, but then trying to address any particular one of them who was not eating her vegetables or was feeding the dog under the table, must have been very confusing.

Or What If they didn't like each other quite enough to consider marriage but they came up with a power-sharing arrangement whereby Louis the 17th would get to be King for five years, and then Napoleon II would get five years and so on. I know that sounds just a bit like a recipe for disaster, but it's not that different to how most political systems in the world work at the moment, with a new government being voted in and out every three or four years or so.

Or What If they just continued the feuding of the previous King and Emperor and the power playing just goes on and on and on, distracting them from important issues within the colony?

We could choose any of those paths and play out the story accordingly. But the What If path we are going to follow involves very momentous events that are about to change everything in the colony big time.

(And I haven't forgotten, there is still that big battle I promised you).

CHAPTER 36

Upsetting the delicate balance of power

But first a quick detour, as there are still some very interesting What If paths that we haven't explored.

For instance, What If the Dutch decide they want an Australian colony too. I mean they already had most of the very early sightings of the continent by Europeans under their belt. And What If they send a few ships over to set up a colony called New New Amsterdam (yes, there was already a New Amsterdam in America)?

And we can imagine that both the English and the French become very worried about that, because it will seriously upset their delicate balance of power. They are both worried that the Dutch will team up with the other one against them.

What to do? What to do?

Well let's presume the Dutch build their settlement in South Australia, because all their maps tell them that Western Australia has too much desert and too many flies. So they find a nice spot in South Australia and start acting all snooty to the British about not having any convicts there, and start acting snooty to the French about all the theatres and canals they build.

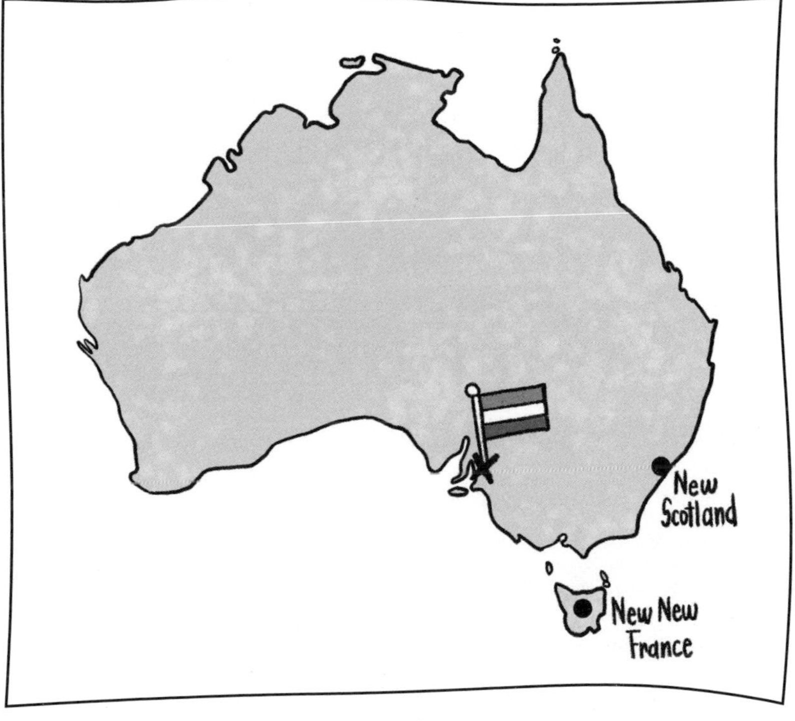

Well What If rather than the all-too-obvious What If story of the French and English forming an alliance to stop the Dutch settlers – What If we do something different? What If the English dress up as French to attack the Dutch, knowing the Dutch will blame the French and then attack New New France in retaliation? And What If, at the same time, the French dress up as British and attack the Dutch, knowing they will blame the British and team up with the French to attack them?

You can picture the French army landing to the east of New New Amsterdam and the British army landing to the west of the settlement. The two armies start encircling the settlement – and they meet up somewhere to the north of it. Things get pretty confusing, of course, as the English think they've met some real Englishmen and the French think they've met some real Frenchmen.

You can see how it plays out, can't you. Both sides presume that their generals have changed their mind about a sneaky attack and have sent in some regular troops without telling them. So both sides hide in the bushes waiting for the other one to attack first.

One English officer peers up over the bush he's hiding behind and asks a junior officer, 'I say old boy, can you see where our regular troops have gone?'

'Yes,' he says. 'I believe I can see their red coats in the trees over there.' And he points. The senior officer points his telescope in that direction and says, 'Ah yes. Now I see them. I wonder what on earth they are doing? They seem to be just sitting there.'

'Perhaps waiting for nightfall for a surprise attack,' says the junior officer.

'Good thinking,' says the senior officer. 'I think we should pull back a little so as not to get in their way then.' And he orders the troops to fall back a bit.

And the senior French officer, sitting in a tree with his telescope pointed at the British troops in French clothing says to his junior officer. 'Mon Dieu, our regular forces are withdrawing. Why would they be doing that?'

'Should I send a runner to ask them?'

'Non, non, it is clear that we are not meant to mix.'

'Perhaps they have received some intelligence about the Dutch forces and need to regroup?' says the junior officer. 'Or perhaps their attack has been called off?'

'Why would it be called off?'

'A peace treaty? The Dutch are going to pay for peace maybe.'

'Ah, true,' says the senior officer. 'If that is the case our generals would not want us attacking until after they have the peace payment from the Dutch. And maybe some cheese. The Dutch make quite good cheese.'

'It would have to be a lot of cheese to call off an army,' says the junior officer.

'Maybe they have thrown in a set of dinner plates and steak knives?' suggests the senior officer.

'Oui,' says the junior officer. 'You can make a very good deal in this land with steak knives.' And then, 'So what should we do?'

'I suggest we pull back too. It wouldn't do for the Dutch to catch us here dressed as Englishmen if there is a peace treaty being negotiated.'

'I'll order the men back to the ships,' the junior officer says.

And so ends the sneaky attack. Sorry if you were expecting a big battle scene just here in the story, but there's still a bit of time...

So now we have three powers on the continent, all jealously guarding their borders against each other. None of them are sure who to best form an alliance with against the other.

And then Spanish settlers show up in northern Australia!

No, I'm not kidding you on this. The Spanish had explored the eastern coast of New South Scotland back in 1793.

In real life, two ships had shown up at the colony of Port Jackson, led by Alejandro Malspin and Jose Bustamante y Guerra. And just like that crazy Frenchman Francois Peron, they too drew up an invasion plan. Instead of relying on the Irish convicts rising up in rebellion though, they proposed bringing troops across from Peru and taking the entire population of the colony prisoner. That would have been about 7,000 prisoners, who they would have then shipped over to South America to be slaves or skilled migrants.

The plan was quite close to being carried out too – except the situation in Europe meant the Spanish had to concentrate their forces on what was happening there as a result of the French Revolution.

But in our What If story the Spanish set up a colony in what is now Queensland, called Nuevo Nuevo Madrid. This is followed by a lot of diplomatic missions between the French and English and Dutch and Spanish to try and establish sensible borders between their settlements and they sign endless friendship treaties and make political promises about not really attacking each other, and things finally sort of settle down to some level of stability. Well, no worse than that in Europe.

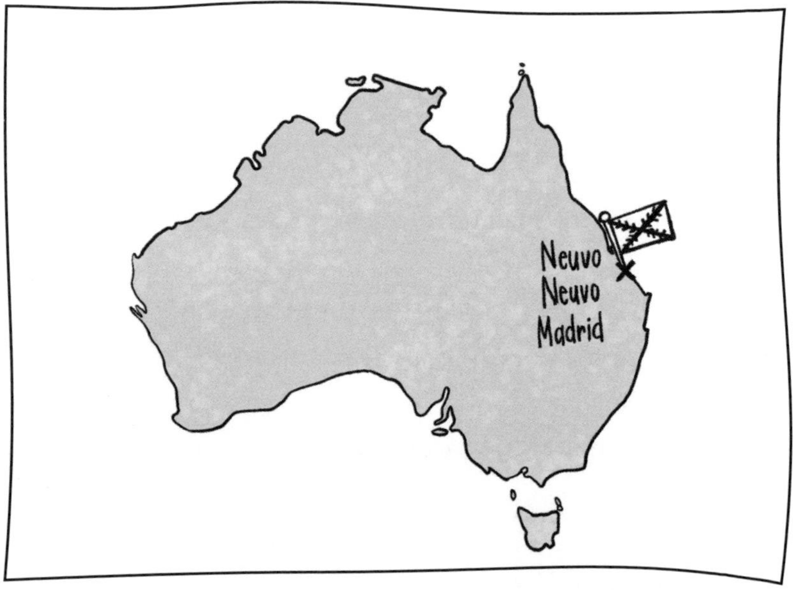

Until a small fleet from Luxembourg arrives looking for a place to set up a settlement…

CHAPTER 37

Back to the main story and that big battle I promised

Okay, enough fun exploring sidetracks, let's get back to the main story. I had promised you some momentous events. And that can really be summed up in one word. Gold.

Goud in Dutch.

Oro in Spanish.

Or in French.

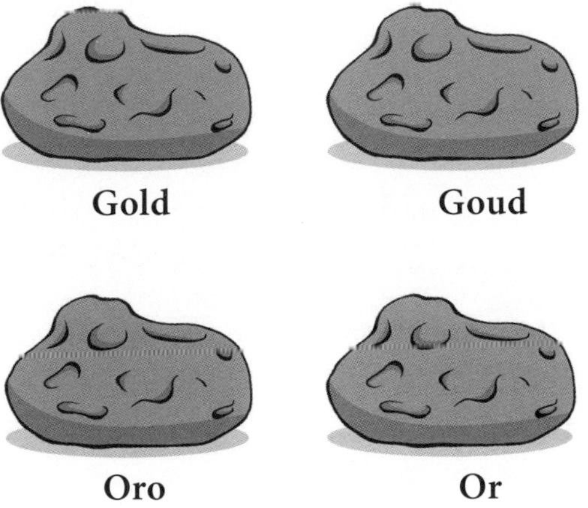

Yes gold had been discovered in New South Scotland and in New New France (sorry New New Amsterdam and Nueve Nueve Madrid), and everything suddenly changed.

Everything.

There is a long, long What If story to explain how this all occurs – which will make a good book in its own right – but to give you the short summary of it all, this is what happens. Both colonies have a sudden influx of people from all over the world, pouring off ships and making their way overland to the goldfields.

Very soon the settlements are no longer just French or British speaking, as people have come from all over the world. Particularly from England and Ireland and China, but also from Sweden and Germany, Portugal and South America – and from Luxembourg!

The colonial governments are first a little bit worried about this, but then discover it is a great way to make a bit of easy money. They can tax the miners. Whatever gold they dig up, the administrators get their cut without ever getting up from their comfy chairs or getting dirt under their fingernails. And you can tax them as high as you like. What is not to like about that?

At least that was the idea – but they soon find that if they raise their taxes too high, the miners all just tromp across the border to the other colony.

But, as things turn out, the gold deposits in New New France prove larger than those in New South Scotland, and slowly more and more miners move south of the border river. And eventually there are more English and Irish settlers in many parts of the colony than there are French.

And we should all know that history teaches us that when you get a minority that becomes a majority – things tend to get very awkward for the ruling power – as we will see. Particularly if they are busy considering other things than internal dissent.

For instance, as the settlements grew richer their dependence on France and Britain grew less, which led to people asking the question – why don't we become independent like the USA? Why don't we declare a free republic here?

And in some areas, like north-east New New France, where there is a large population of Irish settlers, who have settled the largely unsettled land and started farming it – they start asking the same question. Why shouldn't they declare themselves independent of New New France.? Why not declare a free republic here?

And into that comes an agitator who hates the French almost as much as he hates the British. With a gang dressed in iron armour he takes on the French authorities and triggers an uprising. His name is Edward

Kelly – and that's a What If story that is really, really, really interesting, if I do say so myself. And it includes a big battle – which I'd tell you about except we have run out of pages.

So that will have to be a whole other What If story for another day.

Timeline and alternative history timeline

Real history	Year	What If History
Captain Cook charts the east coast of Australia	1770	Captain Cook hits the Great Barrier Reef and his ship sinks
Marc-Joseph Marion Du Fresne lands in Tasmania, and is then killed in New Zealand	1772	Marc-Joseph Marion Du Fresne claims Tasmania for France
First Fleet arrives at Botany Bay. La Perouse arrives too and then disappears	1788	La Perouse claims Louisville in New New France and returns to France
French Revolution begins	1789	French Revolution begins
	1789	Royalists leave France to settle in New New France
King Louis the 16th and Marie Antoinette attempt to escape France and are captured	1791	King Louis the 16th and Marie Antoinette escape to New New France
King Louis the 16th and Marie Antoinette are executed	1793	

Real history	Year	What If History
Napoleon marries Josephine	1796	Napoleon marries Josephine
Napoleon becomes leader of France	1799	Napoleon becomes leader of France
Napoleon declares himself Emperor	1804	Napoleon declares himself Emperor
Napoleon divorces Josephine and marries Marie Louise	1810	Napoleon divorces Josephine and marries Marie Louise
	1810	English First Fleet arrives at Botany Bay, then moves north and establishes New South Scotland
Napoleon invades Russia	1812	Napoleon invades Russia
Napoleon defeated and exiled to the island of Elba	1814	Napoleon defeated and exiled to New New France
Napoleon escapes exile and returns to France and raises and army but is defeated at Waterloo	1816	Louisville/Napoleonville tensions in New New France
Napoleon exiled to St Helena	1815	
	1817	Attempted French invasion of New New London
Napoleon dies in exile	1821	
	1825	Napoleon and King Louis the 16th die in New New France, triggering new power struggles

About the Author:

Craig Cormick is an award-winning author and science communicator, with a special interest in history. He has lived in Iceland and Finland and has travelled to Antarctica four times – though he really prefers the tropics. He has written over 30 books for adults and children, and he enjoys messing with history just about as much as history enjoys messing with him. Craig has been shortlisted for the Aurealis Award in 2018 & 2017; Vic Community History Award - shortlist 2018 and winner 2015; ACT Publishing Award 2015 and many more.

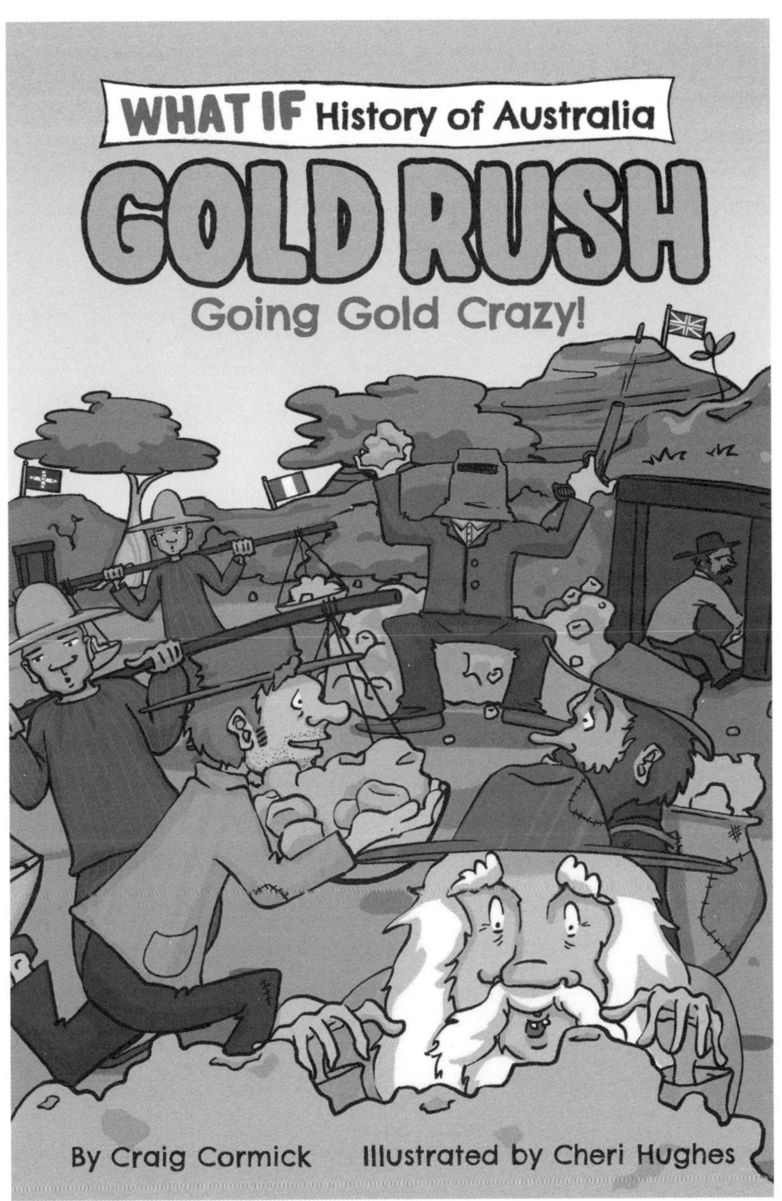

www.bigskypublishing.com.au